DESPERATELY SEEKING DOREEN

Jackie Harris moves from Suffolk to Sussex with her parents, who have decided to open up a guest house, the Mare Vista. She's left her boyfriend Adrian behind, so she doubts she'll stay long, just wanting to make sure her parents settle in. Then an interesting guest, artist Tom Grant, comes to stay. But when she discovers he's not doing much painting — and is doing a lot of creeping around — she begins to wonder what his real intentions are . . .

FRANCESCA CAPALDI

◆

DESPERATELY SEEKING DOREEN

Complete and Unabridged

LINFORD
Leicester

First published in Great Britain in 2020

First Linford Edition
published 2021

A catalogue record for this book is available
from the British Library.

ISBN 978–1–4448–4806–9

Published by
Ulverscroft Limited
Anstey, Leicestershire

Printed and bound in Great Britain by
TJ Books Ltd., Padstow, Cornwall

This book is printed on acid-free paper

Guest Appearance

'And that was David Cassidy, number seven in the chart this week with 'Could It Be Forever' . . . '

Jackie Harris carried on singing the song as the DJ chatted, swirling her rubber-gloved hands around the bubbly water as she washed the last of the cutlery. Her sister Denise had only just left for school and would be in a right mood if she realised she'd missed hearing her idol.

Jackie wondered if Adrian had his radio on at his office, 140 miles away, in her old home of Ipswich. If he did, it would be tuned to Radio 3, so he could listen to something classical.

'Could we have the Home Programme on for a change?' Iris Harris's cheery voice filled the kitchen as she entered. She popped a cup, saucer and plate on the side of the sink. 'Sorry, Mrs Furst's

1

only just finished her breakfast.'

'That's OK. And Mum, it's called Radio 4 now.'

'It'll always be the Home Programme to me. They might have something on about the Duke of Windsor. Such a shame about his passing.'

Jackie finished off the last of the washing up and tipped the water out of the bowl.

'Haven't we someone new arriving today?'

'Yes, a Mr Grant, staying for three weeks. Arriving at five this afternoon at Littlehampton station.'

'Another retired widower, do you think?' They'd had a couple recently.

'If he is, he's a young one. I took the booking over the phone, though you can't always tell. Have you got a shift at the funfair today?'

'Yes. Nine till four. I said I'd meet Val outside here at ten to nine so I'd better get going. I'll be back to collect Mr Grant from the station and I'll help with dinner.' Jackie shrugged the rubber gloves off. 'I'd better move.'

She was about to head up the stairs from their basement living area.

'Jacqueline?' her mother called.

'Yep?'

'The job at the funfair, it can only last the summer. It's as if you're only here temporarily, like the guests.'

Jackie walked back to her mother, putting her arm round her shoulders.

'I only said I'd give it a go here. Mr Brown's keeping my old job open as he can get temps in over the summer period. I don't want to settle down too much in case I decide to go back to Suffolk. And then there's Adrian.'

'Ah, Adrian. I wondered when he'd rear his ugly head.'

'Mum!'

'Well, it's not like he's proposed or even seemed that upset you were going.'

Had he been upset? He wasn't good at showing hurt feelings. He'd certainly been annoyed. He was currently waiting for her to 'come to her senses'.

'No-one's ever good enough for me

according to you,' Jackie joked. 'But whatever I decide, it'll be my choice, won't it?'

'Of course, love. You're twenty-four now, you can do as you please.' She kissed Jackie's forehead. 'And what you decide will be fine with your dad and me, though we'll miss you if you decide to go back to Ipswich, and so will Denise.'

Jackie laughed, recalling her sister's tantrums at the idea of moving to Little-hampton.

'She was the one I thought would have the most trouble.'

'And look at her now. Group of new friends, getting on well at school.' Iris looked at her daughter hopefully.

'And who knows, maybe I'll get to like it here, too. See ya later!'

She swung her bag over her shoulder and took the stairs two at a time. She knew she had a lot of soul searching to do.

* * *

4

'The ghost train wasn't very busy,' Jackie said, as she and her friend Valerie walked out of the funfair building later that day.

'No, neither were the dodgems. Never are on a Monday.'

They made their way past the helter-skelter and the other outside rides until they reached the promenade. Sauntering past the kiosks on the left, selling beach gear, ice-creams and souvenirs, Jackie and Valerie looked out to sea.

'It's good to get some fresh air after being cooped up indoors. Are you off home now, Val?'

'If only. I've got a shift at the Blue Sea restaurant, as one of the waitresses likes to get home for when her kids get in from school.'

'Don't you do a stint at the Nelson on Mondays, too, Val?'

'Yeah. Monday's a busy day for me. It's all extra dosh, though, isn't it? You do your bit at your parents' guest house, so it's not much different.'

Jackie felt immensely lucky. She had the luxury of taking time off her 'real'

5

job, as Adrian had referred to it, to help her parents out and do a bit of seasonal work. She knew that last winter, with the seaside businesses shut, Valerie had done shifts in a couple of pubs. Then there'd been the Saturday job at the Fine Fare supermarket.

'Why don't you get a full-time job?' Jackie asked.

'Oh, blimey, you sound like my mum.'

'Sorry.'

Val giggled.

'It's OK. To be honest, I don't know what I want to do. I left the girls' school, where your Denise goes, with A-Levels, and thought, what next? Mum wanted me to go to Bishop Otter College in Chichester to do teacher training, but I didn't know if I wanted to be stuck with that. Or with anything else.'

'I guess I was the opposite when I left school.' Jackie emitted a sigh that came up from her platform sandals, remembering when she was at that same stage. 'I did want to go to college. Mum and Dad were certainly keen.

'But Adrian didn't want me to go, so I didn't. Dad's best friend runs a factory, so I worked there as a clerk, filing and so on.' She stopped suddenly, recalling the lost opportunity, as one of her teachers had put it. 'Adrian said he'd take care of me, what with having such good prospects, and that when we married me having a career would be pointless.'

Valerie wheeled round to face her, tossing her brown hair behind her shoulders.

'So you're hardly one to talk, are you? Are you going to do shifts at the funfair and the guest house for ever? And this Adrian you talk a lot about, he sounds a bit of a control freak to me.'

Jackie was offended by this analysis. 'He's not that bad! He's been very good to me.'

Valerie tilted her head to one side.

'Sorry, Jackie, I didn't mean to upset you.

But it looks like we both have some soul searching to do.'

Jackie gave her a grin.

'It's all right. One of the things I like about you, Val, is that you're honest with me.'

Valerie beamed at her.

'Yeah, too honest for my own good, Mum tells me.'

They started off down the prom once more, coming to where there was a huge swathe of grass on the left, and beyond that South Terrace, with its Georgian and Victorian edifices. One of them was Jackie's parents' guesthouse, Mare Vista.

'So, if you could do anything, what would you do?'

'What — apart from being an actress like Judy Geeson?' Jackie said.

'Ha, ha, yeah, you wish!'

'Strangely enough, I quite fancied teaching, too. Art. But now, I don't know. I'll probably go back to Ipswich, take up my old job and get back together with Adrian. I do miss him.'

'You good at art, then?'

'I was. Haven't done any for years.'

Valerie was quiet for a few moments.

'I'd better head back to the river and

think about my next shift,' she suddenly said.

'OK. See ya Wednesday.'

'Yeah, see ya.'

Jackie watched for a few seconds as Val headed back in the direction of the pier. She'd managed to keep all these questions she kept asking herself under wraps for the last couple of weeks. Now Val had given her things to think about once more. But at this moment she needed to get back to pick up their new guest.

* * *

The train pulled out of Angmering-on-Sea station and Scott Grant realised it was only one more stop to his destination. Would he find what he was looking for in Littlehampton? His heart thumped against his ribs in anticipation, but also in fear.

As they passed a gas tower and houses came into sight, he shook himself. It was the end of the line. He stood to remove his case and the bag of equipment from the parcel shelf.

On the platform he found a trolley, and loaded it up before walking down to the station entrance hall. It was only then it occurred to him he had no idea who was coming to meet him.

Scott looked towards the waiting room on one side and the news kiosk on the other. A young woman caught his eye. She had on denim flares, a bright yellow smock top and cork-soled platforms. Her hair was tied up in a bright tie-dyed scarf. She was striking, even from this distance. She turned and waved, before running over.

'Are you Mr Grant?'

It was a few moments before he could reply, taken aback by her huge blue eyes.

'That's right. Call me Scott.'

He offered a hand and she shook it firmly. Her touch spread a warmth through his body. Daft. He didn't even know her.

'I'm Jackie, Iris and Stanley's daughter. The car's outside.'

He followed her out to the forecourt.

If everything else turned out to be a disappointment, she at least would be a bright spot. Perhaps he might even paint her.

Jackie opened the boot of the car, then tried lifting his backpack off the trolley.

'Goodness, this is heavy. What do you have in here?'

'Careful. It's my art equipment.'

'You're an artist?' She seemed interested in this. But then people always were.

'That's right. Here, let me pack the car.'

Only minutes later they arrived on South Terrace. She parked outside a tall Victorian red brick house with a double front. The sign said *Mare Vista*. Yes, this would do nicely for the duration of his stay.

No sooner were they in the hallway then it was filled by a welcoming committee. Apart from Jackie's parents there were three guests, long term apparently, calling introductions and wishing him a happy stay.

A teenage girl, introduced as Jackie's sister, slumped against the wall in a navy blue school uniform, clearly there on sufferance.

'Nice to have another youngster about the place,' an old lady with a cheerful round face and a blue rinse remarked. She introduced herself as Mrs Furst, and the Yorkshire terrier in her arms was Archie.

'So what are you here for?'

This kind of nosiness he could do without. No point starting off on the wrong foot, though.

'To draw and paint.'

'For pleasure?'

'He's an artist,' Jackie said.

'Oh, how delightful!' Mrs Furst beamed at him. 'You've come to a good spot, hasn't he, Archie?' She looked at the dog as if he was going to give a reply.

'That's right,' a rather posh, middle-aged woman called Rita Watt said. 'Seaside, river and two completely different beaches. And if you get a chance you simply must get out on to the South

Downs.'

Moustached Raymond, in a cream suit and blue cravat, nodded firmly in agreement.

'We can give you lots of recommendations. So, are you a successful artist?'

'Dear me, let the poor man get his breath and settle in,' Iris said, for which Scott was grateful.

Jackie's father helped him to the second floor with his luggage. It would be a trek up and down with his stuff, but worth it for this view. He peered out of the bay window, across the expansive lawns to the sea.

Away to the right was a large round pond. Behind it was the huge white building of the funfair. Further west was the River Arun. To the left was the massive Beach Hotel, which he'd considered booking. No, this would be better, more intimate, if not more anonymous. And cheaper.

'Dinner's at six-thirty,' Jackie told him.

'Oh. Yes. Thank you.'

The door closed and he was at last

alone. He hoped the rather starchy couple and Mrs Furst weren't going to pester him. He needed this time alone to work out how he was going to locate what he had lost so many years ago.

The Search is On

'Hold on, Adrian, there's someone at the door.' Jackie felt relieved to have a short break from Adrian's long lament over the telephone, for that's what it had become.

She opened the door to Val, beckoning her in and pointing to the phone. She indicated towards the guest sitting-room on the left and went back to her conversation.

'Sorry about that . . .'

'Was it necessary to cut me off? Whoever it was could have waited, surely.'

'It was my friend, Val. We're going out this evening.'

'I don't know why you're bothering making friends when you're not staying.'

'Adrian, I'm not sure what . . .'

'And where are you going? Not out with some chap, I hope.'

'Of course not. Though we are supposed to be on a break.'

'So you can sort out this stuff with your parents, not to date other people.'

15

They hadn't made any specific stipulations. Not that she had any inclination to find another boyfriend.

'We're going to a party, someone Val knows. It's their birthday, I think. Anyway, I need to have a bit of life outside of work.'

'Work!' he barked. 'Is that what you call skivvying for your parents and playing at the funfair?'

'Adrian, I'm not sure this conversation is going anywhere. Besides, I can hear a guest coming down the stairs.'

'Jackie, I'm sorry . . .'

In a louder voice she cut the call short.

'I'll speak to you later. Bye.'

The new guest, Scott Grant, appeared at the same time Val reappeared from the guest sitting-room, presumably alerted by Jackie's strident farewell. He had a sketchbook and pencil case tucked under one arm.

'Hello, Scott.' Jackie put a smile in place as she always did for the guests. 'Is everything OK?'

'Everything's fine.' He grinned in

16

return, dimples forming in his cheeks. That, with the curls twisting to his neck and the green eyes, made him someone she definitely would have looked twice at on the street. In other circumstances.

'It's a lovely evening so I thought I'd get out to do some work. I was wondering where might be a good place to sit and sketch the water.'

His words gave Jackie a brief moment of nostalgia for her lost artistic dream. She was about to reply when Val butted in.

'It's nearly low tide now, so the sea's way out. The river's low, too, but if you sit on the wall opposite the cafés in Pier Road, or go to the pier, you'll get a view of it.'

'What's the quickest way to get to the pier?' he asked.

Val gave him quick and precise directions, adding that the funfair was where she and Jackie did some shifts. He listened intently, nodding every now and again.

'Thank you. You both look like you're

17

dressed up to go out on the town.'

'Just off to my mate Stuart's party,' Val said.

'Have fun.' With that he twisted open the door catch and let himself out.

No sooner had the door shut behind him, than Val turned to Jackie.

'He's cute. Do you think we should have asked him along?'

'Would Stuart want you to invite all and sundry?'

'Stuart's laid back. It's open house as far as he's concerned.'

'Even so, no. He's a guest here and that's business. It's like crossing a boundary.'

'Spoilsport!'

There was a clatter up the stairs, and soon Denise was in the hall.

'Mum says you're going to a party. Can I come, too?'

Val laughed. 'You're too young.'

'I'm fifteen-and-a-half,' she announced crossly.

'Like I said, too young.'

'I thought you went to that disco at

the Trades and Labour Club on a Friday.' Jackie said.

'Yeah, well, I do. But it's boring.'

'Why's that?' Jackie asked.

Denise shrugged, looking glum.

'Just is.'

'Sorry kiddo,' Val said. 'When you're older. Hey, what's that bruise on your arm?' Denise looked down and pulled at her T-shirt sleeve. 'That's huge, Den, and purple. How did you do it?'

Denise looked heavenward.

'I fell over at school and knocked it on a chair. I've got two left feet, OK?'

'Honestly, Den.' Jackie nudged her friend. 'Are we going to this party or not?'

'You bet.'

'I guess you can't wait to see Stuart,' Jackie ribbed her friend, knowing she always denied any attraction.

'We're just friends!' Val protested. 'I keep telling you that.'

Denise pulled a face.

'I don't like Adrian. He's a weirdo.'

'Denise!' Jackie admonished. 'And

what's he got to do with anything?'

'You were on the phone to him. I heard you.'

Val laughed.

'I'm with you there, kiddo.' She opened the door and went ahead down the steps to the gate.

Jackie gave her sister a look, the kind their mum often gave them, before following her friend.

Heading down the steps, Jackie admired Val's purple and white striped flares, teamed with a lilac vest and white platform clogs. She felt rather boring in comparison, having gone for her green check, cotton maxi dress. It hardly mattered since she wasn't going there to find a boyfriend. The thought helped her relax.

Jackie's mind went over Adrian's phone call. No, she wasn't going to let the guilt spoil her evening out.

★ ★ ★

Val hadn't been joking about Stuart's place being an open house. The kitchen and dining-room were full of people chatting, whilst the living-room accommodated the dancers. Jackie was standing in the kitchen, holding a glass of cider, rooted to the spot with shyness. She was listening to Val chat to Stuart about Deep Purple's latest album, unable to offer any insights.

She looked around, wondering if anyone else looked awkward. No, she seemed to be the only one. From the living-room 'Smoke On The Water' was blaring out, which had probably prompted her friend's conversation in the first place.

'Hi, I'm Gary.'

Jackie spun round in alarm, having felt the tap on her shoulder before the voice spoke.

'Sorry, didn't mean to startle you.'

There, grinning, was a young man with blond hair down to his waist. He was wearing scruffy flared jeans and a blue T-shirt.

She must have stared a little too long

at him.

'What, have I got two heads?' he asked, laughing.

'Sorry, it's been a long day,' Jackie said, by way of explanation.

'I'm Gary. What's your name?'

'Jacqueline. That is, Jackie.'

'Well, watcha, Jacqueline, that is, Jackie. How'd ya like a dance?'

Val, who must have heard the exchange, leaned over to Jackie.

'He won't bite, you know.'

'No,' Stuart said. 'He's my brother and he's harmless enough.'

'Thanks for that unflattering compliment,' Gary said.

'Well, are you going to take the lady to dance? If not, I will, and you can keep Val company.' Stuart raised his eyebrows twice.

Gary held his hand out towards Jackie.

'Have fun.' Val sounded mildly put out. Maybe she'd hoped Stuart would ask her to dance.

Jackie weighed up the situation quickly. She had a boyfriend. But no, she didn't exactly. And it didn't matter, because it was just a dance. Why should she assume this guy was interested in anything else?

She took his hand and let herself be led through the crowds to the living-room. It was better to dance with him and have someone to talk to than stand like an idiot listening in to someone else's conversation.

It was then she panicked. When had she last danced at a party, other than a smooch with Adrian? He didn't like dancing to anything but slow records.

The last time she'd been out to a club with friends was six years ago, when she was still at school, moving to the likes of the Kinks, the Beatles and Dave Dee, Dozy, Beaky, Mick and Tich. Too late now, she'd have to copy what Gary was doing. Far from being 'cool', she felt a right freak.

Gary, in the middle of the crowd, closed his eyes as if in a trance. He moved his feet from side to side, swaying his body. He was not a good dancer. Part of her was relieved, but the other now didn't know what to do.

It was then Val appeared on the make-shift dance floor with Stuart. Jackie started moving, keeping her eyes on Val, who nodded approvingly. Gary opened his eyes in time to see Jackie getting into the dancing.

'Great moves!' he shouted over the din.

* * *

Gary had been good company, dancing then chatting, telling her about his job as a car mechanic, asking her about life in Ipswich.

T Rex's 'Metal Guru' was blaring out in the living-room, making it difficult for her to hear what he was saying, even though they were standing in the kitchen.

'Sorry, I didn't catch that,' she told Gary, squinting her eyes and leaning her ear towards him.

'I asked if you have a boyfriend.'

Oh heck, what was she supposed to

say to that? Pretend again she hadn't heard and hope he gave up?

'No, she hasn't,' another voice shouted.

'Are you interested?'

Jackie swung round to see Val there, face determined.

'Well, it's not exactly . . . ' Jackie started, but didn't know how to finish.

'Surprising?' Val offered. 'Considering you've only been here a couple of months?'

Stuart leaned over the breakfast bar.

'We're going to the fleapit tomorrow night. Why don't you two join us?'

'The fleapit?' Jackie's eyes widened with disgust. 'What on earth's that?'

'He means the Palladium Cinema on Church Street,' Val said. 'It's the local nickname. They're showing 'Frenzy'. Do you fancy it?'

'Yeah, cool, man,' Gary said. 'I like a bit of Hitchcock.'

Was this meant to be some kind of double date? But then, Val always insisted there was nothing but friendship between her and Stuart. And what would it look like if she said no?

'OK.'

Val looked at her watch.

'We'd better split. We've gotta be bright-eyed and bushy-tailed for our shift at the funfair in the morning.'

Relief flooded Jackie. She'd wondered how early she could get away from the party, as fun as Gary's company had turned out to be.

'It's a shame, but you're right.'

Gary lurched towards her and she was afraid for a moment he was going to kiss her, but he gave her a pat on the shoulder instead.

'Been nice meeting you, Jacqueline, that is, Jackie. See ya tomorrow.'

'Nice meeting you, too.'

Valerie and Stuart hugged lightly. Jackie noticed Gary pinch up his lips and wondered whether that's because he'd wanted to do the same to her.

'Gary seems a nice guy,' Jackie said as they made their way home. 'But, well, I don't want to be pushed into a date with anyone.'

Val's platforms clip-clopped at a faster rate as she speeded up.

'Who said anything about a date? We're going out as mates, to see a film. What's the problem?'

'So Gary and I are supposed to play gooseberry to you and Stuart?'

Val tutted.

'There is no 'me and Stuart', I've told you that. And even if there were, and I was trying to set you up with Gary, which I'm not, are you really going to continue with the part-time sort of romance that isn't a romance with Adrian? Who, incidentally, sounded like he was giving you hassle on the phone today.'

'You shouldn't have been listening.'

'I couldn't avoid it. If you don't want to come tomorrow, just say.'

Did she really want another Saturday night in, watching 'A Man Called Ironside' and 'Parkinson' with her parents?

'Of course I'll come. I'm on evening meal duty tomorrow, but I can swap with Denise who's doing Sunday, as long as I add a sixpence to the favour. She'll be cock-a-hoop about that.'

They crossed over by the roundabout where they parted company.

'See you tomorrow, then,' Val said. 'Yeah, see you tomorrow.'

* * *

Scott's stomach lurched as he knocked at the seventh door in Southfields Road. It hadn't become any easier with each house. So far an older lady and a younger one with children had helped fill out his 'survey'. Another household hadn't answered the door, whilst the fourth, fifth and sixth had told him, with various degrees of politeness, to go away. Somewhere down this road was a Doris Parks, but it seemed less and less likely he'd find out where.

The door he was now in front of opened slowly and an old gentleman peered out.

'Can I help you, young man?' he said, his voice croaky.

'Hello, sir, my name's Scott and I'm

doing a survey for a company hoping to set up locally. I'd like to ask you a few questions to ascertain what interest you might have in our product.'

The old boy didn't look convinced.

'What you trying to sell then?'

'Artwork. Drawings, paintings. Whatever people are interested in.' He'd picked this as it was, after all, his field of expertise.

'I can't afford that kind of stuff, specially the prices you lot charge,' the man said. 'I'm on a pension, you know. I make do with my family photographs.'

Scott felt immediately guilty. The man was right. Not everyone could afford to decorate their houses with artwork. It had been a stupid idea to pick on this.

'I'm sorry to have disturbed you, sir. I'll make a note of what you said. It's a good idea to make artwork affordable. Thank you for your time.'

'Good day to you, young man.'

Scott made his way back down the front path, hearing the door being shut behind him. On reaching the gate he heaved out a huge sigh. What now? It was pointless carrying on. All he was doing was annoying people. Even if he found Doris Parks, she might not be who he was looking for.

He walked back down to the main road and pulled the map out of his bag. There was the other name he'd found, Dora Perkins. It was closer to the name he'd been given anyway. He checked the address: Beaconsfield Road.

He searched the map for several minutes, sitting on a wall with it on his lap, using a finger to guide himself round. Finally he spotted it. It was almost the other side of town.

He checked his watch: 5.45. He needed to get back to the guest house and get ready for dinner at 6.30. He was jolly hungry, too. He'd forgotten to eat at lunch time because he'd been concentrating so hard on examining the local newspaper at the library.

He'd have to admit defeat today, he realised with great disappointment. He'd been here five days and had got virtually nowhere. He only hoped his luck picked up in the next two weeks.

A Rare Night Out

Jackie caught sight of herself in the long hall mirror as she rushed by. The green eye shadow complemented her hair and contrasted with her blue eyes. The emerald flares and striped tank top over the white blouse seemed to strike the right chord, making it look like she'd made an effort, but not tried too hard to impress.

She opened the door and poked her head out to see whether it was still raining. Not only had it stopped, the sun was peeping out of the clouds as it hung in the sky over the river. Behind her she heard masculine footsteps clumping down the stairs.

It was Scott.

'You look nice. That colour suits you.'

'Thank you.' She picked up her corduroy jacket from the hat stand.

'Off anywhere interesting?'

Was he hoping for an invite? Or was she simply hoping he'd find her fascinating enough to want to accompany her somewhere?

'To the pictures with a group of friends.' Going with Scott rather than Gary suddenly became appealing to Jackie. Tough luck, since she didn't have the choice.

There was a knock on the door so she twisted round to open it. On the doorstep were Val, Gary and Stuart.

'And here they are,' she said for Scott's benefit.

'Watcha, Scott,' Val called, giving a little wave.

Scott lifted his hand in greeting.

'Watcha. Anything good on at the flicks?'

'Hitchcock,' Gary replied.

'I'll tell you whether it's worth seeing tomorrow at breakfast,' Jackie added, still wondering whether he was angling for an invitation.

'Have a good time,' Scott said, before heading to the dining-room for dinner.

'Your brother?' Gary asked when they headed down the steps.

'A guest. He's an artist, here for three

weeks to paint.' Not that he'd produced any evidence of that.

At the Palladium they bought tickets for the stalls and settled themselves in. Jackie had been hoping to sit next to Valerie, with Stuart and Gary either side, but it wasn't to be. She was at one end, next to Gary, who was next to Val with Stuart on the other side. An unease set in as she considered the possibility of Gary trying to kiss her in the dark. What would she do?

The lights dimmed and the B film started. It was another thriller, but not particularly thrilling in Jackie's opinion. She heard whispering to her right. Gary and Val were giggling about something, almost certainly one of the many ridiculous moments of the film. Gary didn't share it with her, which irked her a little. He made no attempt even to put his arm around her, which was a relief, even if it made her question what was wrong with her.

As the lights went up after the B film had finished, Jackie glanced towards

Stuart and Valerie. It didn't look like they'd ended up in any kind of embrace either. Maybe that's why her date hadn't tried anything.

'Ice-cream, everyone?' Gary stood and shuffled past her. 'My treat.'

'I'll give you a hand,' Stuart offered, following on.

They headed up to the usherette standing near the exit, with her tray of ice-creams and orange squash containers, managing to be first in the queue.

'You all right?' Val asked.

'Why wouldn't I be?'

'You weren't keen to come.'

'I wasn't, but I'm looking forward to 'Frenzy'.'

'Well it couldn't be any worse than that B film. Z film, more like.'

They were laughing at some of the more bizarre moments when the men returned with four tubs of vanilla ice-cream.

Jackie had just finished hers when the main feature began. There were several incidents in the film that made her jump.

On one occasion she grabbed hold of Gary's arm without thinking, immediately regretting it in case it gave him ideas. But he simply turned to her.

'It made me jump, too,' he whispered.

She wasn't used to seeing creepy films at the pictures. Back in Ipswich Adrian had usually dictated what they saw together, and they'd tended to be war films like 'Zulu' or 'Battle of Britain'. When she'd gone with girlfriends, very occasionally, they'd picked lighter films and comedies. It made her realise how narrow her life had become.

By the end she was relieved it was over, though Val and Gary had clearly enjoyed it. Stuart declared it not as good as some of Hitchcock's other films. They left the cinema and headed back down Church Street.

'There's time to go to the Spotted Cow before last orders,' Gary announced.

'Count me out,' Stuart said. 'I'm bushed.'

'Me, too,' Jackie said quickly, afraid that Valerie was about to say the same

36

and leave her alone with Gary. 'I've been busy in the guest house all day and I'm due to help with breakfasts early tomorrow.' She thought that would put an end to the whole idea until Val spoke.

'I'll come with you, Gary,' she piped up. 'Let these spoilsports get to their beds.'

Gary looked first at Jackie, then Stuart.

'Do you mind?' he asked.

'Course not,' Stuart said quickly.

'Fine by me,' Jackie said. 'I'll see you Monday for work, Val.'

'Perhaps we could all meet up sometime next week,' Stuart suggested.

Gary and Val carried on down to East Street, Stuart going with them to catch the bus. Jackie, relieved to be making her own way home, only hoped Val wasn't upset about her spoiling her plans to get her together with Gary. He was a nice guy. He just wasn't the guy for her.

★　★　★

Valerie hadn't called for Jackie on Monday morning, phoning to say she was running a little late and she'd see her at break time. Jackie hoped that's all it was, and that she wasn't still annoyed about Saturday.

Her morning with the ghost train went slowly, there being little custom. She was glad of her 15-minute break at 11 o'clock, going immediately to the grassed area outside, around the Oyster Pond. It had long given up its original purpose, instead housing several pedal boats for people to hire. Jackie was sitting with her back against one of the tall trees.

'Hi,' Val called.

'Hi.' Jackie sat next to her friend, opening her flask to share the tea as she always did.

'Ta,' Val said, as she took the plastic inner cup from Jackie.

'Sorry about Saturday evening. I seriously couldn't have stayed awake much longer.'

'No sweat. Gary and I had a ball. We

went back to his after and played records till about two in the morning. He has a great LP collection.'

'Does he live at the house in Courtwick Lane?'

'No. Only Stuart still lives at home. Gary's got his own place. He earns decent money, what with owning the garage and that.'

'I didn't realise it was his business.'

Valerie looked at her askance.

'Would that have made you keener?'

'No, of course not.' Oh, dear, Val really was off with her for leaving early. 'I'm glad Stuart and I leaving didn't spoil the evening.'

'Nope, it certainly didn't.'

Val immediately started on a different subject, firstly local gossip then moving on to the Duke of Windsor, whose burial was happening that day. Jackie had the firm impression the subject of Saturday was now off limits.

As soon as she'd finished the tea, Val handed the cup back to Jackie and jumped up.

'Better get back. See ya later.' She'd soon disappeared round the corner. There was still five minutes to go.

Yes, Val was definitely irritated about something.

* * *

'So, what have you liked best so far on your holiday, Mr Grant?' Mrs Watt called from the window table in the dining-room.

Scott, just finishing the last of his toast took a while to reply.

'Well, I like the contrast of the two beaches, pebbles and sand. Both interesting to draw. The river's attractive. And there are some rather intriguing flint buildings in the town.'

'Goodness!' Mrs Furst exclaimed. 'Haven't you been out of the town yet, lad? You've been here a week.'

'Um . . .' Scott shrugged. He could feel his face heating up.

'That won't do,' Mrs Watt said. Her dark pencilled eyebrows were more arched than normal.

'Do you hear that, Jackie?' she called over as the young woman came into the room with a pot of tea. 'Scott's not been outside Littlehampton yet.'

Jackie looked over at him in surprise. 'Really? Not even to Arundel?'

'Not yet.' He wasn't about to admit he'd spent much of the time in the library and walking round the town.

'You're in luck,' Mrs Furst said, leaning down to give Archie a sausage. 'It's Jackie's day off.'

'Oh, I wouldn't . . .' he started.

Jackie put the pot on Mrs Furst's table.

'I was planning on going into Arundel today. Why not tag along? If you like.'

It would be churlish of him to turn down the offer. Besides, he rather liked the idea of Jackie's company.

'OK. It'd be good to be shown around by a local.'

'I'm not a local but . . . I'll explain later. Can you be ready for ten?' He nodded.

'Bring your sketchbook if you like. There'll be lots to draw.'

41

An Awkward Call

Jackie thought Scott might not be up for walking the four miles to Arundel along the river bank, but it turned out he was a keen hiker. They were a quarter of the way there now, strolling in companionable silence. The muddy green water was rushing past them as they reached a bend.

The sun disappeared from time to time behind the strip of cloud that marred the blue sky, but it didn't affect the warmth of the day. She wasn't sure what had possessed her to volunteer her day off, but she wasn't exactly regretting it.

Scott looked more relaxed today in jeans instead of black trousers, accompanied by a stars and stripes T-shirt and corduroy jacket.

'You mentioned you weren't a local,' Scott said, breaking into her thoughts. 'I must admit, the accent's been puzzling me. West Country?'

'West Country? Certainly not!' She

laughed. 'My parents moved here from Ipswich in January, after buying the guesthouse. They opened at Easter. I've taken some time off my job there to help out in the initial months.'

'So you're not staying?'

Jackie's stomach flipped as the complication reared its head once more.

'I really don't know yet. I'm an office clerk in Ipswich. I could do that anywhere, I suppose, but . . . I just don't know.'

Scott stopped, turning in a circle.

'The view here's wonderful.'

'I've been doing this walk since I was little. Dad came from Littlehampton originally and we used to visit my grandparents.'

She copied him, twisting round to take it all in, the river and the verdant plains. In the distance Arundel Castle and the Cathedral were nestled in a crease of the South Downs with the rest of the town.

'Would you like to stop and draw?' She pointed to the black canvas bag on his shoulder.

'I brought my camera instead,' he said, lifting it out. 'That way we can keep moving and I can get lots of images to work with later.' He put the strap round his neck, using a light meter before he snapped several photos.

She was disappointed she wouldn't see him work.

'I hope you have plenty of rolls of film, the rate you're taking those.' She laughed.

'I do.' He smiled at her, his eyes kind of blue, yet also green — like the sea when the sun shone on it. She looked away, embarrassed by the jolt of attraction.

'Come on, plenty to see further on.' They enjoyed a lunch of omelette and chips in a small café in Arundel and the time had passed pleasantly. This was followed by a brief glance round the paintings in the art gallery opposite.

Scott had replied precisely to her questions about his time as an artist and what he liked to paint. She hadn't explored why he'd chosen to spend time in Littlehampton. And what would he have said if she had?

After, they'd walked to Arundel Castle, a few minutes away. Scott had been fascinated by the edifice, with its mixture of older and more modern buildings, looking at it with his artist's eye.

They made their way to the top of the castle and were standing now on the walls, peaking through the battlements. There was a warm breeze blowing her hair. The people below looked like beetles scurrying around.

'I never tire of this view,' Jackie said.

The River Arun snaked its way along the plain, into the distance. Beyond, the sea was lost in a pale haze.

'We're lucky it's so clear today.' Scott took several photographs. He turned the camera in her direction. 'Do you mind?'

'I . . . suppose not.' She smiled stiffly, trying to pose.

'Just be yourself.'

She laughed.

'Easier said than done under instruction.'

'Tell me what Ipswich is like. I've never

been there.'

She did as he suggested, her face relaxing as the words flowed. There were several mentions of an 'Adrian'. A boyfriend? What was that to him? He'd be gone in three weeks, tops.

'Are you going to paint me, then?' She laughed.

He raised his eyebrows.

'It's a possibility.'

'I was joking.'

'I'm not. Perhaps I could paint you as a princess, standing aloft a tower, looking into the distance. You would be waiting for someone.'

'Gosh, and I think I've got a vivid imagination! Waiting for who, exactly?'

He shrugged.

'A prince on a white steed?'

She pulled a face.

'Hmm. I don't need a prince to rescue me. I'm perfectly capable of looking after myself.'

'I'm sure you are.'

Jackie leant against the stone. The breeze rippled the purple smock she was wearing over corduroy jeans.

'Are you waiting for someone, then?'

He came to.

'What? Oh, aren't we all waiting for someone special?'

'I already have someone. Sort of.'

Of course, Adrian.

'You said you were a clerk in Ipswich. But what would you really like to do?'

She chuckled.

'It's funny because Val asked me that recently.' She hesitated. 'I wanted to be a teacher originally, but ... I just didn't do it.'

'What kind of teacher?'

'I'm not sure I should admit this to you.' She gave a nervous giggle. 'An, um, art teacher?'

'Is that a question?'

'No. I just feel a little inadequate confessing that to a professional artist.'

He straightened up, looking her in the eyes.

'Do you still draw or paint?'

She slumped a little and sighed.

'Not really. Work got in the way.'

'Perhaps we could take some sketch pads down to the beach one evening, do some sketching.' The idea appealed to him no end. Still, he didn't want to put her under any pressure.

'Maybe,' she said.

His thoughts turned to Adrian, this sort of sweetheart or whatever he was. He felt the need to get to the bottom of the relationship.

'Must be hard, having a boyfriend so far away. Sorry, I'm assuming that's who Adrian is.'

She puffed out her cheeks and blew out a long breath.

'He was. Though I guess it's kind of on hold.' He gave a brief nod to acknowledge what she'd said.

'How about you?' she asked. 'You implied you're waiting for someone. So no girlfriend?'

'No girlfriend currently, no.'

'Come on,' she said, 'we've got Arundel Park to do next. We'd better get on.'

'After you, Your Highness.'

She laughed again and led the way.

48

Arundel Park had been a favourite of Jackie's when she'd visited her grandparents as a child. Entering by Swanbourne Lake now, she longed for those untroubled days of her childhood. She pictured Granny and Gramps, striding ahead, beckoning her on. They always had liked a good country walk.

The lake, to the left of them, was surrounded by trees, with a wood extending into the park on one side.

'Shall we take a walk first?' She pointed up the path, to the gently rolling South Downs beyond.

'First? Before what?'

She pointed to the lake.

'Taking a boat out.'

'Ah.' He looked out at the line of rowing boats bobbing up and down on the ripples.

'You're not afraid of water, are you?'

'Of course not. I'm sure it'll be fun.'

Their conversation around the park was general, keeping away from anything personal.

Back by the lake, Scott volunteered to

row. Leaning her head back and closing her eyes, Jackie breathed in the warm air. A group of mallards swam past them, quacking at the intrusion on their habitat.

The sun bounced off the water, making the scene dappled and hazy, like a dream.

She'd enjoyed her day out with Scott much more than she thought she would, and certainly more than she'd intended. Maybe, on her next day off, she could drive him more deeply into the Downs, or show him vibrant Brighton. She reprimanded herself. It was ridiculous to entertain thoughts of future outings.

'It's amazing how well a warm, sunny day makes you feel,' she said, sitting up straight. 'I guess it's a change from being indoors.'

'You should get out more, then.' She laughed.

'Between working at the funfair and the guesthouse, there's not that much time.'

'I guess not. That's the advantage with my job, I guess, though I don't think of it as a job. More a vocation.'

They both went quiet once more, distracted by their own thoughts.

Scott's mind drifted. If history had been different, he might have been here with HER in the boat. He wondered what she looked like now, what colour her hair was. He tried to imagine Jackie was her. A bit too young, of course.

A sadness enveloped him. Best not to trawl through the 'what ifs' and terminated possibilities. Yet wasn't that why he was here?

'Look out!' Jackie lunged forward, grabbing the side of the boat.

'Ooh, sorry.' He'd nearly run into the small island in the middle. Taking charge of the oars, he soon propelled them around and away from the bank.

'Phew, sorry about that,' he said. 'I was miles away.'

'Thinking about that 'someone' you're looking for?' she teased.

He grinned but said nothing. If only she knew how close she was.

By the time they got home, Jackie was confused.

'I'd better go and help Mum and Dad with dinner now,' she told him, opening the front door to the boarding house.

'Thank you for a most enjoyable day. I really should try and get out of Little-hampton and bit more often. It's just there's . . . so much here.'

She gave him a questioning look.

'Really?'

'From an artist's point of view, that is.'

'Oh, yes, I suppose so.'

'If you have any other recommenda-tions, or fancy a day out, you know where I am.' He treated her to a beaming smile.

She wasn't sure how to take that. Part of her wanted to clap her hands in delight and sort out a day here and now, but her sensible side urged caution. Where would this be going?

Rita and Raymond Watt sauntered down the stairs, chatting about the weather.

Seeing Jackie there, Rita smiled.

'We're just popping out before dinner for a quick walk. Hello, Mr Grant.'

'Had a good day in Arundel?' Raymond asked.

'It's a lovely place,' Scott replied.

'It certainly is. Rita and I have been a few times. See you at dinner.'

After they left, Jackie turned to Scott.

'I'll have to think about some other places you can visit.' She wouldn't commit either way to the other suggestion.

'That'd be good.'

He headed upstairs as she took the steps down to the basement.

'Hello, dear,' her father said, turning from the sink where he was washing up.

'Nice day out?'

'Yes, gorgeous weather for it, too.'

'And our artist friend?' Iris asked, chopping a carrot.

'He enjoyed Arundel. Took lots of photos of the castle. Think it appealed to his romantic soul.'

'He's a romantic, is he?' She raised her eyebrows and gave a cheeky grin.

'As an artist, that is. Honestly, Mum.'
Jackie didn't want her getting any ideas.
She would do anything to make sure
Adrian was history.

'Shame.'

'Where's Denise?'

'Doing her homework in her room.'

'Listening to her record player, more
like,' Stanley said.

'And what can I do to help?' Jackie
looked for the tea-towel to dry up.

Stanley tipped up the bowl to flush
the water down the sink.

'Nothing, it's your day off. Go and put
your feet up, or watch the telly.'

The phone rang in the hall upstairs.

'I'll get it,' Jackie offered, glad of something to do.

'Take this in case it's a booking.' Iris
handed her the diary.

Jackie took the steps two at a time.
She picked the receiver up and put on
her best receptionist voice.

'Good evening. Mare Vista guest
house, how can I help you?'

'It's Adrian.'

'Hello, Adrian, how are you?'

She was happy to hear his voice, but wished he hadn't chosen now. It felt like he'd found out about Scott and was ringing up to berate her. Silly, of course. It was her own guilty conscience playing on her mind.

'I'm lonely without you. I thought about going to the Langley Arms for a meal this evening, sitting outside by the river, but it wouldn't be the same without you.'

That was sweet of him. Her heart softened.

'You have lots of friends.'

'It's not the same.'

'And,' she started tentatively, 'you could always find a date. Linda at your office has a soft spot for you.'

She felt a pang of jealousy at the thought, but she couldn't begrudge him having some fun.

There was a long silence.

'Adrian?' Jackie prompted.

'I'm here. Just flabbergasted that you'd suggest such a thing.'

'I bet your flabber has never been so ghasted,' she quipped, quoting Frankie Howerd.

'What do you mean by that?' He sounded offended.

'It's a catchphrase, you know . . .'

But she didn't get a chance to finish before he interrupted.

'Can't you take anything seriously? I'm pouring my heart out to you here and you're quoting rubbish.'

'Sorry, I . . .'

'Forgiven. Now, what have you been doing today?'

'I've been to Arundel, showing a guest around.' There was no harm in it so she might as well be honest.

'That's a bit above and beyond what guest houses provide, isn't it?'

'I didn't mind because I've been meaning to go there for a while. I used to go with Granny and Gramps.'

'I hope she appreciated you giving up your day off, this guest.' This was the moment to explain, or it would have been if Adrian hadn't spoken again straight away. 'When are you giving up this fantasy and coming home?'

'Adrian, it's not a fantasy. I'm helping Mum and Dad out. And I'm trying to work out what to do with my life.'

'You don't need to. You've got me.'

'Not at the moment. We're on a temporary split.'

'Only because we're not close enough to see each other. You're just being childish. What on earth can you do in Littlehampton that you can't do in Ipswich?'

Things that aren't always decided by you, she thought.

'I've yet to find out, Adrian. And you know what they say — absence makes the heart grow fonder. It might do our relationship some good.'

Iris came up with some cutlery.

'Still on the phone?' She didn't wait for an answer before hurrying to the dining-room to lay the tables. She must have realised who it was.

'Your mother, by any chance?' Adrian knew he wasn't her favourite person.

There was a knock at the door. Jackie

noticed three shapes through the frosted glass.

'It's like Piccadilly Circus in here,' her mum said, coming back into the hall to open the door. 'Oh, look, it's friends come to call for you,' she said extra loudly.

'Friends?' Adrian questioned.

'Yes, Val from work and some others,' Jackie replied.

Iris peered out at them.

'So who have we here?'

'Gary and Stuart.' Val pointed to each in turn.

'Gary and Stuart,' Iris repeated, the volume up a notch more.

Jackie put her hand over the receiver.

'Mum!' she mouthed.

At the same time, Adrian spoke.

'Who are Gary and Stuart?'

'Friends of Val's,' she replied.

'I see.'

'Look, I'd better go, see what Val wants.'

'But I wanted to ask you to come up to Ipswich next weekend, for a party.'

'I can't at the moment, Adrian. I'll ring

you tomorrow, when I have a moment.'

'Make sure you do. Not like last time you said you would.'

'OK. See ya.' She replaced the receiver.

'I'll leave you to it,' Iris said.

'Wondered if you'd like to come out for fish and chips and a walk by the beach,' Val said.

'I did say I'd help with dinner.'

Stanley appeared, carrying a tray of starters — half a grapefruit with a glacé cherry on top. At the same time, Scott appeared round the corner of the stairs.

'You take yourself out, Jacqueline,' Stanley said. 'I told you there was no need of your help.'

'You sure?'

'Absolutely. Hello, Scott. Starter is served.'

'Hello again.' He waved at the group.

Would Scott think either Gary or Stuart was her boyfriend? She needed to stop feeling guilty about everything. Scott wasn't her boyfriend, and neither was Adrian at this moment in time.

'I'll go and fetch my bag,' she told Val.

'Have a good evening out,' Scott said, as she was about to go downstairs again.

'Thanks, Scott, I will.'

He disappeared into the dining-room and she continued down the stairs.

Denise's Secret

Jackie had enjoyed her evening out with Val, Gary and Stuart. They'd bought fish and chips on Pier Road from the Blue Sea. Sitting on the wall opposite to eat them, they watched the river as it flowed rapidly towards the sea.

Afterwards, they'd headed to the fair for rides on the Merry Mixer, Waltzer and the dodgems. It made a change to go there as a customer instead of an employee.

Jackie thought about this as she helped with the post-breakfast washing-up the following morning. Out with Scott, out with Gary, on the phone to Adrian, all on the same day. Any onlooker who didn't know any better would think she was stringing these three poor men along.

She had a momentary panic. Was she, in fact, leading them on? If Gary had been interested, surely he'd have made his move at the cinema. Jackie had made the situation clear to Adrian. As for Scott, there was nothing going on there. A nice day out with an interesting person who shared a love of art with her. Full stop.

'Will you stop daydreaming and get those dried up?' Iris said. 'I'm running out of space on the draining board.'

Jackie came to.

'Sorry. I was miles away.'

'So I could see. Was it Gary or Scott you were thinking about?' She grinned as she scrubbed the frying pan.

Oh, dear, Mum didn't think she was stringing them along too, did she?

'There is no Gary or Scott, not in the sense you mean.'

'I'm only kidding. I'm glad to see you've made friends. It's not always easy when you move at your age. It's different when you're at school, like Denise. There's a class full of potential friends.'

'Perhaps. I'm glad I didn't move when I was at school, though. Somehow I think that would have been more of a wrench.'

Mum placed the pan on the drainer.

'So leaving Adrian wasn't so bad, then?'

'I didn't mean that. I meant . . .'

What did she mean?

The phone rang in the hallway above.

'I'll get it,' Stanley's voice called down.

Jackie was glad of an opportunity to change the subject.

'Why don't you get one of those dishwashers? It would save us doing it.'

'They're very expensive. Why spend the money when we can do the job, and probably better?'

Stanley tapped down the stairs, a worried frown marring his usual jolly countenance.

'That was Denise's school. They wanted to know what's wrong with her as she hasn't turned up in the last week.'

'What?' Iris exclaimed. 'They must be mistaken.'

'Apparently not. Where on earth has she been going if not to school?'

'I don't know,' Jackie said. 'But strangely we were just talking about the stress of moving schools. Perhaps she hasn't settled in.'

'But she claims to have made loads of friends,' Iris said.

'The school said she's the only one missing from class,' Stanley told them.

Jackie thought a while.

'Unless she's made friends outside school.'

Iris slammed the washing-up brush into the caddy.

'I know what this is about. I bet there's some boy involved who she's been playing hooky with.'

Stanley shook his head.

'We don't know that. She's a bit young for boys, isn't she?'

Both Jackie and Iris looked at him in surprise.

'She's fifteen, Dad.'

He sighed.

'I suppose she is. Doesn't seem five minutes ago she was a little girl playing hopscotch and cuddling teddy bears.'

Iris grabbed her side and sucked air in through her teeth.

'What's wrong, love?' Stanley asked. 'Have you got indigestion again?'

'I suppose so. Funny place for it. Must have eaten something that didn't agree with me.'

'Perhaps you should see the doctor. You've had that a while now.'

'See the doctor for a bit of indigestion? I'd be laughed out of the surgery. It's probably all this worrying over Denise.'

'Don't worry about that now, love. We'll tackle it when she gets back.'

'It might be a good idea to hear what she has to say first,' Jackie suggested.

Iris recovered from the stab of pain.

'There's no excuse for missing school.'

'Even so, Jackie's right. Let's hear the girl out first.'

* * *

'Watcha Mum, watcha Dad!' Denise's cheery voice rang clear down the stairs, alerting Jackie, Iris and Stanley to her arrival home, just after four o'clock.

The three of them looked at each other.

'Remember, let's play this cool,' Jackie said.

The click clack down the stairs of Denise's platform clogs was heard just before she appeared.

'Nice day at school?' Stanley asked.

'Yeah, ace, ta.'

'So, what lessons did you have today?' Iris could barely keep the simmering irritation under wraps.

Jackie was afraid her mother's pout and narrowed eyes would give the game away before they intended. But Denise didn't seem to notice.

'What we always do on Wednesdays.'

'What's that then?' Iris persisted. 'I haven't memorised your timetable.'

'Do I have to go over it? It's so boring. And it's hot outside and I feel whacked.' She slumped into a dining-chair and laid her head on her arms.

'You said your day had been 'ace' a minute ago. Make your mind up.'

Stanley stepped forward.

'Let's get you a nice cold drink. That'll pick you up a bit.'

'No, we're going to sort this out now!' Iris barked. 'You haven't been in school

66

for over a week.' She slapped her hand down on the table.

Stanley put an arm around his wife.

'Iris, calm down, please.'

So much for playing it cool. Jackie stepped in, even though she'd resolved earlier to let her parents deal with it.

'Denise, where have you been today? We've been worried sick. The deputy headmistress rang this morning. You haven't been in school since last Monday.'

Iris lifted her hand and pointed a finger at her younger daughter. It started wagging as she spoke.

'If you're not careful, you'll be leaving the end of this school year and won't even be doing your O-Levels. Never mind your fancy ideas of staying on for A-Levels. I'll put you to good use here.'

Denise bolted upright.

'I don't care, because school is rubbish!' Her voice finished the sentence in a shriek.

Stanley stepped forward.

'Don't you use that tone to your mother, my girl. Now where have you been, and who have you been with?'

Denise folded her arms tightly across her chest, creasing her lips into a tight pout. She studied the wall rather than look at anyone.

'You never did this in Ipswich, so someone's leading you astray,' Stanley persisted.

'Was it someone from another class in your year?' Jackie asked her sister. 'Or an older girl? Someone telling you she'll . . .'

'No!' Denise shouted.

'Oh, I get it.' Stanley scraped his hand through his thinning hair. 'It's a boy-friend.'

'No.' Denise pulled her arms around herself even tighter.

'Don't you go protecting him,' Iris said. 'He should be at school too. Unless . . . Oh, Denise! He's not . . . older, is he?'

Denise unfolded her arms and leant her hands on the table.

'There is no boyfriend. There's no-one at all!' By this time she was shaking. 'I don't have any friends in this dump. All my friends are back in Ipswich. I told you I didn't want to move here. I told you!'

Denise collapsed on the chair once more.

'Oh, sweetheart!' Her mother plunged forward, taking her daughter in her arms as she sobbed into her mother's shoulder.

Jackie and Stanley looked on, her father's face a picture of remorse.

When the crying subsided, Denise explained a little more.

'I haven't made any friends since I got here. They take the mickey out of my accent and say I'm thick.'

'What accent?' Stanley looked confused.

'Did you tell a teacher?' Jackie asked.

'No. The girls said they'd beat me up if I did. They'd already slapped me and pushed me about. And they followed me home and said they knew where I lived so I wasn't safe anywhere.'

Jackie remembered the bruise Denise had explained with a fall.

Iris let Denise go, keeping hold of an

arm.

'You should have told us. This is terrible. I'm going to phone the school right now. And one of us will run you to school each day.' She took a cotton hankie from inside her sleeve and handed it to her daughter.

Stanley looked forlorn, shaking his head as he came forward to place a comforting hand on Denise's shoulder.

'I'll ring them,' Jackie said, aware her parents were too upset to approach the problem calmly. 'Hopefully someone will still be there.'

She headed up the stairs, composing her speech in her head as she went.

Jackie Makes a Decision

Jackie and Val sat on the wooden boat as it chugged over from the western to the eastern side of the River Arun. They were returning from a sunny afternoon off on West Beach, it being a half day at the funfair for both of them. They'd alternated swimming in the still cold sea and relaxing among the grassy dunes in the sun.

'Was Denise going back to lessons today as well?' Val asked.

'No, she's only going in to talk things through with the headmistress. She'll go back tomorrow.'

'Poor thing. Kids can be so cruel.'

'Can't they just.'

'Are you thinking of having another day out with Scott next week?'

The mention of his name gave a surprising jolt to her heart. Embarrassment, most likely.

'How did we get from Denise to Scott?'

Val grinned and raised her eyebrows.

'You've gone red. Didn't you say he'd suggested you had another day out?'

'No. He only said if I fancied a day out, I knew where he was.'

'You should take him up on the offer. He is a dish.' Val giggled, tucking her long curls behind her ears.

Jackie couldn't argue with that. But . . .'

There is something bothering me.'

'What's that?' Val asked.

'I haven't seen much evidence of this sketching he claims to do.'

'Artists can be rather precious about their work.'

'He takes a lot of photos, though.'

'Really?' Val scrunched up her brow. 'Isn't that a bit creepy?'

Jackie wished now she hadn't mentioned it.

'It's probably nothing. He says he uses them for his sketches, so I guess he needs lots.'

'I'd keep an eye on him. Hey, perhaps he's a private investigator.'

Jackie laughed.

'That at least would be exciting.'

They arrived at the other side of the river on to Pier Road, passing the row of cafés before turning on to South Terrace.

'It was nice of your mum to ask me in for afternoon tea,' Val said as they took the eight steps up to the front door.

They'd only just entered the hall when Iris came running out of the dining-room, a pink pinny tied round her waist.

'There you are, Jackie. You have a visitor.' She didn't seem particularly happy about it. Whoever could it be?

As she stepped into the dining-room, Adrian stood up from one of the tables.

'At last. I thought you'd never get here.' He was attired in a suit and tie that were far too warm for the day. His hazelnut hair was cut even shorter than normal.

She should have kissed him in greeting, but was embarrassed by his curtness. She bit back a sharp retort.

'Adrian. This is Valerie. Val. A friend I made at the funfair.'

He ignored Val's outstretched hand.

'You've still got your little job then?'

'It gives her a bit of extra money on top of what I pay her,' Iris said stiffly.

Mum didn't like Jackie's job, either, keen for her to get something full time in Sussex, but she was fond of contradicting Adrian.

'Come on, Valerie, sit down.' Iris pointed to the table. 'And you, Jacqueline. I'll be bringing up the sandwiches soon.'

Jackie sat next to Adrian, and Val next to her.

The front door opened and shut. Iris went into the hall.

'Scott,' they heard her say, 'you're just in time. Do join us for afternoon tea.'

What on earth was Mum thinking?

Iris led him in, ushering him to the prepared tables laid up with white cloths, cutlery and flowers.

'This is a friend from Ipswich, Adrian Carter,' Iris said.

'A friend of Jackie's, actually,' Adrian said, caressing her shoulder.

Scott put his hand out.

'Scott Grant,' he said but as before, Adrian ignored it. Scott took a seat opposite Jackie, raising his eyebrows ever so slightly. She looked away.

Adrian held court, detailing his 'horrendous journey', until Iris and Stanley brought up the sandwiches and teapots and joined the others at the table. Denise was the last to enter, bringing another plate of sandwiches. She plonked herself on the remaining chair at the end.

'Have you told Adrian about your trip to Arundel, showing Scott around?' Iris inquired.

Adrian glared at Scott.

'No, I've not heard about this.'

What was her mother up to? Jackie would have stern words later.

'Scott hadn't a clue where to begin so I thought I'd show him some of the sights.' Jackie shrugged as if it were no big deal. 'It was Mrs Furst's idea, really,' she added quickly, glad she'd remembered that detail.

'Is that so?' Adrian helped himself to

75

a ham sandwich, laying it on his plate. 'And what is your business here in Little-hampton, Mr Grant?'

Anyone would think Scott was being interrogated. Why had her mother made things worse by inviting him for tea?

'I'm an artist, Mr Carter. I like to visit different landscapes, to draw, get ideas.'

'I've never heard of you.'

'Not yet, anyway,' Iris interrupted.

'And have you found anything of interest here?' Adrian glanced at Jackie.

'Seaside light always makes objects appear a little different.' Scott picked up a tinned salmon sandwich and took a bite.

'You're lucky Jackie was still here to be a guide,' Adrian said. 'I'm sure she'll be back in Ipswich soon, won't you, darling?'

Adrian took her hand, squeezing it a little too hard, as if displaying ownership. He leant sideways to kiss her cheek. She had the urge to laugh as she noticed Denise screw up her nose.

'Nothing's decided yet,' Jackie said,

worried that she was losing control of the situation.

'No, and I think we should leave the decisions to Jacqueline, don't you?' Stanley said pointedly.

'Quite so, quite so,' Adrian purred in his most ingratiating voice. 'But I know where Jackie's heart lies.' He put his arms around her, pulling her into a bear hug. Jackie noticed Scott look away while her mother pursed her lips. She'd missed Adrian's embraces, but didn't relish sharing them with a room full of people.

'Can we hurry up and finish these sandwiches?' Denise said. 'I'm dying for one of Mum's scones.'

★ ★ ★

Adrian left early next day, before Jackie had awoken. Last night he'd become more cheerful, less snappy, when they'd been left alone. They'd gone out for a walk by the beach and river, stopping by the Britannia, on the river's edge, for a drink.

He'd reminded her of the old Adrian, the gregarious, generous nineteen-year-old. Seven years ago, that was. Had they really gone out that long? His earlier displeasure was probably because he wanted her to himself, Jackie realised, rather than surrounded by family and strangers. She should be flattered.

Placing a rack of toast down in front of Scott, the only guest down so far, she felt a pang of guilt. Perhaps she shouldn't have taken him for the trip out. What if he'd got the wrong impression? She couldn't blame Adrian for being a little miffed.

'So, what are you up to today?' Jackie asked him, 'with the weather being dull and a little cooler?'

He finished his last mouthful of cereal.

'Up to?' he asked, blinking.

'It's just an expression.' Now she'd offended him as well as Adrian. It wasn't her week.

'I'll probably head off somewhere to sketch.'

'Perhaps you could show me some of

your drawings sometime.'

'Maybe.' He seemed distracted. She was about to leave when he added quickly, 'I, er, don't suppose, by any chance . . .'

She didn't find out what he was going to say before an anxious cry was heard from the stairs. Iris came flying into the dining-room.

'Jackie, have you seen Denise this morning?'

'No. She's still in bed as far as I'm aware.' Iris pressed her fists against her chin.

'But she isn't. I went to get her up for school. I can't find her anywhere.'

'Sorry, I'd better go and help look for her,' Jackie told Scott.

'Of course.'

Jackie ran up to her sister's bedroom on the second floor, not because she didn't believe her mother, but she had a bad feeling about this. In the room she checked the top of the wardrobe and then inside it.

'What are you looking for?' Iris cried, running in just after.

'Her case has gone, Mum, and some of her hangers are empty.' She checked the drawers. 'And her underwear's gone, too, by the looks of it.'

'Oh, no.' Then something seemed to occur to her mother and she raced off.

Jackie followed her down the three flights to their kitchen, where Iris opened a cupboard door and pulled out a tin. Opening it up she turned it upside down. There was nothing.

'I had ten pounds in fifty pence pieces in here. They've all gone.'

Stanley came in from the back garden with an empty kitchen bin, chatting away, oblivious. Then he saw their expressions.

'What's up now? Is Denise refusing to go to school?'

'Worse,' Iris said. 'She's gone.'

'Gone? What do you mean, gone?'

Jackie explained what they'd found. 'And it has occurred to me . . . ' She could be very wrong about this. She hoped she was. 'Adrian went back to Ipswich this morning.'

Stanley placed the bin down.

'You mean, you think he might have taken her? Surely he wouldn't be so irresponsible?'

'I wouldn't put anything past him,' Iris said. 'Probably getting his own back for you leaving Suffolk and coming here.'

'Mum, please. I'm sure I'm wrong.' Trust her to voice her suspicions. Her mother was bound to jump on it. 'She might have sneaked into his car. If she's even gone with him.'

'We should ring him, just in case,' Stanley said.

'He won't even be home yet. Look, I'll ring at about ten.'

It wasn't a telephone call she was looking forward to.

A voice called down the stairs.

'Hello! Is anyone there?'

'Mrs Watt,' Stanley said. 'I'd better see to their breakfast. After, we'll have a walk round the town. She might have changed her mind about going wherever it was she was planning.'

'I'll see to the guests,' Jackie said.

Iris followed her daughter to the stairs.

81

'I'll ring my sister and ask her to look out for her. If she is going to Ipswich, she might head there.'

In the dining-room, both the Watts and Mrs Furst had come in, along with a couple who'd been staying since Monday and were heading away today.

'So sorry to keep you all waiting,' Jackie apologised.

'Scott here tells us that young Denise has disappeared. Is that right?' Mrs Furst asked.

'It seems that way. She's taken her suitcase. We think she might be trying to get back to Ipswich.'

Scott pushed his side plate away.

'I've finished my breakfast now. Shall I go to the station and bus depot to check? She might still be there, if that's what she's planning.'

A small wave of relief passed over Jackie.

'That would be so helpful, thank you.'

Mrs Furst rose from her chair.

'I'll go and check on the beach.'

'But you haven't had your breakfast,'

Jackie protested. 'We're not going to stop serving. We can't check with people we know in Ipswich till later.'

'No time like the present. You know what kiddies are like when they claim they're going to run away. They don't get far. I remember doing it myself, my little bag packed with impractical bits and bobs.'

'Thank you. We'll get you something to eat when you get back.'

'That'll be lovely. And I know you've got new guests coming today and need to get ready for them.'

Jackie noticed the Watts conferring among themselves before Rita turned to Jackie.

'If you don't mind, we will have our breakfast first. Then we'll check around the town for you. She might be sitting in a café there.'

'I'm sorry we can't help,' the man on the fourth table said, 'but we have a train to catch.'

'That's quite all right.' Jackie felt the tears pricking her eyes because of all the kindness she'd already been offered. 'We've booked your taxi for ten as you requested.'

Back in the hall, Mrs Furst passed Jackie and let herself out of the front door, waving a farewell. Scott hung back.

'This Adrian . . .' he began.

What was coming next? This was hardly the time for enquiring about her relationship with someone.

'What about him?'

'He went back to Ipswich this morning, didn't he? I was wondering . . .'

'We've already thought of that, but thank you. It's unlikely, but I'll give him a ring later.'

'I'll, um, be going then.' He pointed outside.

'Yes. And thank you, Scott.'

'You're welcome,' he said, passing Val as she came up the steps.

'Where's he off to in a hurry?' her friend asked. 'And aren't you ready yet?' She noticed Jackie's apron.

'I'm not going to work today. Could you explain to them at the funfair, please?'

'If I knew what I was explaining.'

Jackie took a deep breath and went through the whole story again.

* * *

Jackie didn't get hold of Adrian until ten minutes after midday, having tried his home and office several times.

'Thank goodness,' she said, when she finally heard his voice.

'It's nice to know you miss me so much, darling.'

Ignoring this, she ploughed on.

'Did you take Denise back to Ipswich with you?'

'I beg your pardon? What on earth are you accusing me of?'

Trust her to jump in without explaining.

'I'm not accusing you, sorry, more asking. Denise has gone, so has her case. I wondered if you gave her a lift up.'

The long silence told her that Adrian was beside himself with rage.

'Why on earth do you think I'd do that without your family's say-so?' he finally growled. 'How irresponsible would that be?'

'Yes, of course it would be. It's just we're frantic. We've had people running around looking for her since early this morning. We've phoned Aunty Brenda but of course if Denise is heading there she won't have arrived yet.'

'She did, of course, ask me for a lift.'

'What? Why didn't you mention it?'

'It was after you and I had already said our goodbyes. She came out the front with a case and asked for a lift. I told her not to be a silly girl and get back inside.'

'But she didn't go back. She ran away! Adrian, you are the giddy limit.'

'I'm the giddy limit? You're the one accusing me of kidnapping.'

'I am not! I only wanted to know if she'd travelled with you.'

'Why on earth are you shouting?' Iris demanded, having just run up the stairs. 'Has she gone with Adrian or not?'

Jackie put her hand over the phone.

'No, but she asked him for a lift.'

'Why on earth didn't . . . '

'I'm dealing with that, Mum!'

'Your mother's in on the act now, is she, no doubt accusing me of all sorts?'

'She also wants to know . . . ' Jackie had the phone snatched from her by Iris.

'I also want to know why you didn't think it worth your trouble telling us Denise asked you for a lift.'

'Mum, let me handle it.' Jackie went to take the receiver but Iris moved it to her other ear.

'I see. And that's your defence, is it?'

Jackie wrested the phone off her mother and stepped back, almost pulling the phone off the table. Iris flew into the dining-room with a duster.

'It's not my fault if the silly girl has no discipline,' Adrian was saying. 'Whose fault is that?'

'Don't talk to my mother like that.' Jackie was shocked by his tone.

'Oh, it's you. She's the one who started it.'

'She's worried about Denise. And she

is right. You should have told us.'

'Look, I'm sorry, OK?'

An apology from Adrian? She realised, hearing it, that it didn't happen very often.

'Could you at least keep your eyes and ears open? Apart from Aunty Brenda, she has friends in the area.'

'You realise this wouldn't have happened if you hadn't moved.'

Not again.

'If no-one ever moved in case their children ran away, it would be a boring and stale old world, Adrian.'

'I need to get to work now. I've already lost half a day with coming all the way down to yours.'

She was tempted to retort with 'I didn't ask you to come down', but knew it wouldn't help anything.

After short farewells Jackie put the phone down and leaned her head against the banister.

'Are you OK?'

She looked up to find Scott coming down the stairs.

'Not really. I was ringing Adrian to see if he, um . . .' She didn't like to admit she'd accused him of driving Denise home, which is what she'd done.

'Knew anything about your sister's disappearance?'

'Something like that. She asked him for a lift, but he refused.'

'And he didn't think to tell you that at the time? She's a kid.'

Scott got it, so why didn't Adrian?

'Anyway, not a lot more we can do at present.'

'I'll go out again in a minute, have a look round. Mrs Furst's right. Kids don't normally go far if they run off. Might she be with a school friend?'

'She hasn't made any, Scott. I think that's why she's run away.'

'Oh, that's sad.'

He was about to say more when they heard Mr and Mrs Watt's voices.

'I'll go and take that look,' he said.

★ ★ ★

By late afternoon they still hadn't located Denise. Aunty Brenda hadn't heard from her at all. Jackie and Iris sat at the kitchen table, compiling a list of Denise's friends in Ipswich, trying to remember their surnames.

Stanley was on cooking duties for dinner, where he was preparing his specialty, coq au vin.

'She's not likely to go to anyone she wasn't good friends with,' Iris said.

Jackie looked at the list.

'Then most likely she'd contact Teresa, Sharon, Janet or Sally.'

'My sister will have her work cut out searching in the directories, since we don't know their father's first names. We're not even sure of Sally's surname.'

'But at least Brenda's going to give it a go. It's good to have someone in the area who can look.'

There was also Adrian, of course, but Jackie couldn't imagine him poring through the telephone directory.

'I'll give her a ring now,' Iris said. 'Who do you think she should start with?'

'Teresa and Sharon, maybe, as I know one of them lives on Belstead Road, and the other on Belstead Avenue. I can never remember which way round it is. Or is that Teresa and Sally?' Jackie tapped her head as if trying to jog her memory.

'One of her friends lives on Wherstead Road, down near the river. No idea if it's one of those four, though,' Stanley piped up.

'We'll add it to the list of possibilities,' Iris said. 'This should get Brenda started, at least. We can figure out the rest as we go along.'

'I think you should give the police a call, too, while you're there,' Stanley said. 'If we can't locate her, we'll need some help.'

'OK.' Iris took the list of names upstairs.

Jackie shivered. Where was her sister now? Would she even know how to get to Ipswich from Littlehampton? They'd always driven down. If she was still in the town, she might feel too embarrassed to come home.

Val had kept an eye out for her at the funfair. She'd rushed over after her shift to say she hadn't spotted her, before hurrying on to her shift at the Blue Sea.

'You all right, love?'

She looked up to see her father's concerned face.

'No. Neither are you.'

'True.' He rearranged the apron and sat down beside her. 'But I'm sure Denise will be fine. She's a sassy little madam, and very bright. If she was heading to Ipswich, I'm sure she'll get there.' He laid his hand over hers.

'That smells good, Dad. No wonder it's a favourite with the guests.'

'And since we have new ones just arrived, I wanted to impress them. So I've also done a pineapple upside down cake.' He pointed to the oven.

'A nice taste of summer. Hope there's enough for us, too.'

'There will be.' He patted her hand and got up.

Pineapple upside down cake was Denise's favourite. As the thought sent her into a depression once more, Jackie came to a sudden decision. Leaping up from the chair she headed upstairs.

Iris's forehead was puckered as she talked quietly into the telephone.

'Jackie's just come up,' she said. 'I'll ask her . . . Aunty Brenda wants to know which of the four is her best friend.'

'I think they were very much a foursome really. But she's known Teresa since junior school, if that's any help.'

'Did you hear that, Brenda? Teresa . . . OK, thanks love. Good luck.'

Iris replaced the receiver, only to pick it up again.

'Mum, I've had an idea.'

'I'm going to ring the police first, then tell me about it.'

Jackie walked round her mum to sit on the stairs, listening to the one-sided conversation that didn't sound that helpful.

Iris put the phone down once more.

'They said to carry on what we're doing and if she doesn't turn up in a couple of days, to ring again.'

'That's not a lot of use.'

'No, but they wouldn't have any better idea where to look than us. They say runaways normally turn back up within forty-eight hours. And since she's fifteen and gone off on purpose . . .'

Jackie shifted herself off the stairs.

'Mum, I've decided to go to Ipswich. I'm sure Aunty Brenda will put me up. I'm quite happy to track down her friends and ask around. Maybe go to her old school and ask the headmaster there to make an announcement, if necessary.'

'I'm not sure.'

'I could head off now. Get a train into London and change there for Ipswich.'

Iris pondered a moment.

'At least wait until tomorrow morning. Let's see what Brenda comes up with.'

Jackie was eager to go now, but she could see the sense of waiting.

'OK.'

'And you'll take the car. It'll be easier to get around once you're up there. You'll have her case to lug back. If you find her.'

Jackie hadn't driven much since she

passed her test a couple of years back, but the idea appealed to her.

'Thanks Mum.' She kissed her cheek. 'I only hope Brenda has some luck.'

All's Well . . .

Jackie arrived at her aunt's just before lunch on the Saturday. Brenda hadn't had much luck the evening before, so Jackie was eager to see how her aunt had got on this morning.

'Good journey, dear?' Brenda picked up Jackie's holdall and carried it into the house.

'Not too bad. A bit heavy going through London but the traffic kept moving.'

'I'll put the kettle on.'

Jackie followed her into the Victorian terrace.

'What's the latest?'

'It's not been easy, with them all having common surnames. You know I only managed to track down Sally's old house last night.

'She was the one on Belstead Road. The family have moved to Lincolnshire and the new people in the house kept the number.'

'Such a shame.'

'I got hold of Sharon's father this morning.' She put the holdall by the stairs and carried on to the kitchen.

'What did they say?'

'Denise isn't there. What's more, he wasn't sure about Teresa or Janet's addresses because Sharon and her mother are staying over with the grand-parents in Norfolk this weekend. And before you ask, they don't have a tele-phone.'

'Oh, dear, we're not having much luck.' Jackie took a seat at her aunt's table.

Brenda pushed the telephone direc-tory towards her niece.

'There are two Smith families on Bel-stead Avenue, but neither of them are Teresa's family.'

'That's a nuisance. Perhaps it was Janet's family who lived there.'

Odd though, as Jackie could have sworn she picked Denise up from there in her parents' car, not long before they moved to Littlehampton.

'I couldn't find any Taylors on Bel-stead Avenue.'

She found the Taylors in the directory and double checked. No, none on Belstead Avenue. There were plenty of others, though. It could be any of them.

'OK, I'd better get started.'

'I'll bring your tea to the hall.'

'Thanks.' She stood to exit the kitchen, then stopped dead still. 'No. Hold on. It wasn't Taylor. It was Tayborn.'

She sat and quickly flicked through the directory once more. Brenda stood over her, peering down as she searched.

'There. Tayborn. And there are only two. Hallelujah!'

'Here, you're all atremble. Let me ring.'

Jackie followed her out. She was breathing rapidly, her head thumping as she watched her aunt dial. Please, please, please.

She listened as Brenda told them she was looking for Janet Tayborn.

'She does? Wonderful.'

Jackie crossed her fingers on both hands. Surely she'd be able to give them some clue.

Brenda explained why she was calling. It was evident Denise wasn't there, but as her aunt spoke to Janet she started smiling and nodding.

'I see. That would explain it. OK.' She picked up the pen on the table. 'Go on.' She scribbled down a number. 'Thank you very much, Janet . . . Yes, so do we. Bye-bye, now.'

Jackie couldn't contain her excitement. 'Well?'

'The reason we couldn't find Teresa in Belstead Avenue is because she moved six months ago, not long after you. The new directory came out about three months ago, so must have their new address in.'

'So where are they now?'

'Woodbridge. That's what, about ten miles away? Here are their details.' Brenda pointed to the address and phone number on the pad.

'Denise never mentioned they'd moved. I'll ring them this time.' Jackie picked up the receiver.

She dialled the number while her aunt stood in the doorway. The ringing tone on the other phone went on for some time. Jackie bit her lip, wondering where to go from here.

'Hello,' a voice finally said.

'Hello, is that Teresa Smith's house?'

'It is.'

'This is Jackie Harris. My family are looking for my sister, Denise.'

'Ah. Didn't you know she was here?'

'No, we didn't.'

'Oh, dear. You'd better come over then.'

* * *

Jackie was glad of Brenda's company on the trip over to Woodbridge. She had no idea how to play this, whether to be cross with Denise for running away or grateful that they'd found her.

'You won't be travelling back with her today, will you?' her aunt said.

'Goodness, no. I'll leave tomorrow, if that's OK.'

'Of course it is.'

At the Smiths' house, Teresa's mother

had opened the door before they'd got up the path. She gestured them in and showed them to the sitting-room.

'I'm so glad you called. Teresa and Denise are in the back garden at the moment. I didn't say anything in case she bolted.'

'So she gave no hint that she'd run away?'

'Goodness, no, I'd never have allowed her to stay otherwise. I thought she'd travelled up with your parents for the weekend, and that they were visiting family. I don't know if Teresa knew.'

'I'm sorry you've been put into this situation,' Jackie said. 'We found out she's been bullied at her new school and was bunking off. Next thing we know she's run off.'

'Oh, dear. I guess she wanted to catch up with a real friend. They've been writing, you know.'

'Yes. I wish Denise had mentioned you'd moved.'

'It would have made finding us easier.'

They chatted for a while about the situation and the best way to handle it.

That is, until there was a high-pitched giggling heard from the kitchen.

The two girls fell into the sitting-room, laughing and holding on to each other. It was a few seconds before Denise registered her sister and aunt sitting there. She jumped back and looked shocked.

'Wh-what are you doing here?'

'We could ask you the same thing, madam,' Brenda said. 'Got your parents and sister in a right two-and-eight, you have.'

Denise sagged and looked at her feet.

'I'm not going back to Littlehampton.'

'Not today, no,' Mrs Smith said. 'We've decided you can stay here the rest of the weekend.'

'We'll be travelling back tomorrow evening,' Jackie said. 'I've got the car with me.'

'I don't wanna go.'

'You can't stay in Ipswich, Denise. You know that. Enjoy your time while you're here.'

Denise said nothing. Her friend held on to her arm and looked glum.

'Well, I think it's time for lunch, girls,' Mrs Smith said.

'We'll get going, then,' Jackie said. 'And see you tomorrow at five. Thank you for holding on to her.'

'You're welcome. She's no trouble at all. Teresa was so excited when Denise rang to say she was coming up.'

'It's been good of you to have her.'

Back in the car Brenda turned to Jackie. 'I'll give Jane and Bobby a call when we get back, invite them and their families round for dinner.'

Jackie recalled long summer holidays as kid, playing with her cousins. They hadn't kept in touch as much as they should have done since they'd all grown up.

'I'd like that.'

A niggling voice told her she should tell Adrian she was around. Then again, she'd only seen him yesterday. This was time for family.

★ ★ ★

Jackie arrived at the Smiths' at five the following afternoon, as arranged. Her sister was already in the hall with her suitcase, mouth down at the corners. Teresa was standing next to her.

'You know you're welcome any time, don't you?' Mrs Smith told Denise.

'And Teresa is welcome to come down to us in Sussex as well,' Jackie said.

The two teens gave each other a tearful hug.

'Keep on writing,' Teresa said.

'Of course I will.'

'Come on now.' Jackie hurried her along.

'I said we'd pop back to Aunty Brenda's so she can say bye to you before we leave.'

Denise ran out to the car, almost sobbing now.

'Thank you again for having her,' Jackie said to Mrs Smith.

'She was no trouble at all. And Teresa certainly enjoyed seeing her.'

In the car, Denise was huddled up in a ball, looking out of the window. Jackie let her be, driving to the aunt's in silence.

When they arrived, Denise was slow to get out of the car, dragging herself up the path to where Brenda was standing in the doorway. Jackie got out but left them to it, having already said her goodbyes.

She heard a car draw up behind hers but didn't bother looking. It was probably the next door neighbours returning from somewhere.

'How long have you been up here?'

Jackie jumped. Adrian was walking towards her, lips scrunched together and a heavy frown marring his forehead.

'Oh, hello, Adrian. Since lunch time yesterday. We found Denise,' she said pointedly, indicating her aunt's house.

'You should have told me you were coming. We could have met up.'

Jackie looked to where her sister and aunt were deep in conversation.

'I didn't come up for a weekend away, you know. I had to find my sister.'

'So where was the ungrateful little madam?'

She wasn't allowing him to get away with that.

'You know, sometimes, Adrian, you can be so insensitive. Denise has been experiencing a hard time at school and wanted to be with a friend. It wasn't a great thing to do, no, but I'm glad that she's safe.'

'I'm sorry, I only meant . . . '

'Not everything is about you, you know.'

'I know, sorry. Can you come for a drink, while you're here?'

'Are you not listening? And no, we're heading off now. I don't want to get home late. I only saw you Friday.'

'I didn't realise it was rationed.'

'I'll come up another weekend, OK? I'll stay with Aunty Brenda and we can do some things together.'

'You could always stay at my flat.'

'No, Adrian, I couldn't. Ah, here she comes.'

'I'll give you a ring tomorrow,' he said, walking away.

She felt like retorting, 'Is that a threat

or a promise?'

'Is that Adrian?' Denise asked as she got in the car.

'Yes. He was passing.'

They set off, Denise curling into a ball again. She dropped off to sleep until they reached the outskirts of London.

'I'm curious,' Jackie said when Denise woke again. 'You said you went for walks and took the bus to Worthing when you should have been at school. But what did you do in the evenings you said you were at the disco, or out somewhere else with your friends?'

Denise sat herself up.

'Just used to wander around the town. Or sit on the beach when it was nice. Play the penny machines in the funfair. A couple of times I went to the Palladium on Church Street.'

'The fleapit,' Jackie said.

'I wouldn't know.' She looked sad again. 'I just picked it 'cos it's more out of the way than the Classic on the high street.'

'It'll be all right now, you know, at

school. The teachers will be keeping an eye out, so the girls won't dare bully you.'

'It still won't mean I'll have any friends.'

'Let's wait and see, shall we?'

Denise leaned her arm on the side window and looked out. Jackie took that as a sign that the conversation was over.

Suspicious Behaviour

When Jackie arrived back at Mare Vista from her funfair shift on Monday, she was eager to hear news of how Denise's day had been. Her sister had looked woeful when she'd set off to school that morning with Mum.

In the kitchen Stanley was making a pot of tea.

'Hello, Dad. Mum and Den not back yet?'

'Hello, love. Not yet. Your mum said she'd take your sister to Fashion Fair in the arcade to get her a new mini skirt and some pop socks. Thought it might cheer her up.'

'That's nice. I was wondering how she got on at school.'

'Me too.'

They sat with a cup of tea and chatted until Iris and Denise were heard coming in the door from the garden.

'Here we go,' Stanley said.

Jackie was glad to see a smile on

Denise's face, though it was likely due to being out of school and the new purchases.

'Did you get something nice?' Jackie asked.

'Yeah, it's really cool, look.' She pulled a purple skirt from the bag and held it up against herself.

'That's pretty.'

'And school was ace today 'cos the bullies had to say sorry and were really told off in class by Miss Bolton. And in the break two of the girls came up to me to make friends.

'They were both new last year and both got bullied when they came. They said they would've made friends before but when they saw me sitting with my head in a book on the field they thought I didn't want to be friends. And they've asked me to go to the funfair at the weekend.'

She was so excited that Jackie wanted to cry with joy. Instead she sniffed back the tears and listened to details of the two new friends, Gillian and Ruth.

After Denise had run upstairs to her bedroom, Jackie took the clean table-cloths upstairs to the dining-room. As she was heading along the hall, Scott came in through the front door.

'Hi,' he said, with a small wave. His camera was slung around his neck. 'How was Denise's day at school?'

Denise's disappearance and the trip to Ipswich had been the talk of the dining-room this morning when she'd been serving.

'After the Headmistress's talk to the class she made a couple of friends. She seems much happier.'

'I'm glad to hear that.'

She was touched by his concern.

'Where have you been today then?'

'Me? Um . . . walking by the river. Just ambling around really.'

'Get any good photographs?' He lifted the camera.

'Time will tell.'

'See you at dinner. I'd better get on.' She'd liked to have kept on chatting, but she had tasks to do.

111

He'd got to the bottom of the stairs when he turned to her.

'Just a quick question, if you don't mind.'

'Go on.'

'Do you, by chance, know a woman in Littlehampton named Doreen Parson? She was, er, someone my mother knew.'

'Has she been trying to contact her?'

'Well, no. My mother's been dead some years. I'd like to make contact myself. If I could. While I'm here.'

'The name doesn't ring a bell, but I can ask my parents. Hold on.'

As Jackie walked away, Scott called after her.

'I don't want to be any bother.'

'It's no bother.'

In the basement kitchen, she put the question to her parents. Stanley in particular considered the name but decided no, it was unfamiliar.

Jackie went back to the hall.

'Sorry, no joy,' she told Scott. 'Are you sure she still lives in Littlehampton?'

'Not entirely,' he admitted.

'Have you looked in the directory?'

'Yes, but there wasn't even a D. Parson in the town.'

'Sorry we couldn't be of any help.'

'Don't worry, it doesn't matter.'

Scott turned once more to go upstairs. The expression on his face belied his words.

★ ★ ★

Scott had been subdued at dinner that evening, and was much the same the following morning at breakfast. Jackie wondered if this Doreen Parson had been a special friend of his mother's. With his mother having passed on, he perhaps felt the need to talk to someone who'd known her well.

As Jackie cleared the breakfast things, she saw him leave the house with his canvas bag.

Stanley came in with the vacuum cleaner.

'You don't have to do that, it's your day off.'

'I'll finish off first, Dad, but thanks.'

She watched Scott through the window. He was standing at the bottom of the steps, opening a book of some sort and peering inside. Remembering the nice day out they had the week before, Jackie rather wished she'd suggested another outing to him.

'What are you doing today?' Stanley asked.

'Think I'll take a walk to Val's first. She's lending me an LP and I said I'd collect it from her house.'

★ ★ ★

Later that morning, coming out of Val's gate, Jackie's eyes were on the artwork of the album she'd borrowed. She stopped on the pavement to flip it over and examine the back. It was then she spotted a figure walking towards the other end of the road.

She watched as the man lingered outside the end house, before secreting himself in a bush.

It was Scott.

What was he doing here and why was he acting so furtively?

She tucked the LP under her arm and scooted down a side road on to Wick Street, running down it until she came to the beginning of Beaconsfield Road, by a school. Scott was still secreted in the bush, but Jackie was now behind him.

She tucked herself into the school entrance and watched him. It wasn't long until he was lifting his camera and taking photos through the gap in the hedge. The reason became clear when Jackie noticed a young woman amble down the path of the first house, which had scaffolding over part of it.

Could Scott be a private detective, like Val had suggested? The idea was kind of exciting. She imagined being his assistant, a Susan Saint James to his Rock Hudson like in the cop series 'McMillan And Wife'. More likely he was stalking this young woman.

Suddenly it didn't seem like a game any more. This morning Scott had asked about some friend of his mother's, presumably a much older woman. So where did this young woman fit in?

His question had seemed harmless enough at the time, but from where she was standing now, his interest had taken on a sinister tone.

Time to ask a few questions of her own.

Scott watched as the young woman walked out of her gate and away in the opposite direction down Beaconsfield Road. Dora Perkins, Doreen Parson. It might be her. He scolded himself for not having the courage to approach her. She looked a little young for the age she would be by now, but people sometimes did.

Scott re-emerged from the bush, watching as Dora disappeared down a side street. What was the point of coming all this way if he was going to do nothing?

Turning to walk back to Wick Street he jumped, gasping noisily as he did so. There, right in front of him, was Jackie.

She looked a mixture of puzzled and cross. It must have looked mighty odd, him hidden in a bush.

'Oh. Hi, Jackie. You made me jump. What are you doing here? Not following me, I hope.' He said it as a joke but saw straight away that he'd misjudged the situation.

'I could ask you the same,' she said accusingly. 'It's hardly a tourist spot.'

'I've been wandering around, taking photos. They're interesting little terraces, with their arched windows and doors. Late Victorian, I think.' That was true at least.

'Taking photos from a bush?'

'Gives them a frame. What are you doing here?'

'I've been to Val's. She lives further up.' She pointed.

'I see. I'm heading back to the guesthouse now. You?' He noticed she was carrying the Yes album, 'Fragile'.

'That's a brilliant record.'

'I haven't heard it yet. We should walk back together.'

To keep an eye on him? She didn't otherwise seem thrilled about the prospect.

'I'll show you the quickest way,' she said.

He liked the idea of walking back with her, but he wasn't finished with his task just yet.

'I'm quite happy to dawdle back,' he said. 'There are some interesting alleyways and paths.'

She shrugged.

'OK. See you later.'

'See ya.'

It was only as she walked away he realised he'd been foolish to mention Doreen Parson earlier. He'd wanted to double check but hadn't thought it through. He gave Jackie time to get well ahead, watching as she disappeared into the distance.

Heading in the same direction, he scooted down a side road that took him back on to Wick Street.

He'd noticed a phone box on his way here. Yes, there it was. He stepped inside, ringing the number he wanted before pushing the pennies into the slot.

'Wimbledon 1957. Kenneth speaking.'

'Hello. It's me. Gotta be quick.' He looked around outside to make sure Jackie hadn't doubled back.

'How are you getting on?'

'I was wondering if you were sure about the name Doreen Parson. Could it have been Dora Perkins?'

'Mmm. It's possible. I did say we couldn't be certain. It was a terrible time and we never met her. We only know what the neighbours told us. They knew very little because she hadn't been there long.'

'OK. I'll give you another ring in a couple of days, in case you happen to remember anything else.'

After a few pleasantries, Scott put the phone down. The coins clunked into place and he pushed open the door. Looked like he'd have to do a bit more digging.

* * *

On her way back to Mare Vista, Jackie thought hard about Scott and what she'd seen. Unless he *was* a private eye of some sort — unlikely — then there was something else going on here he wasn't being honest about.

Val had been right — his obsession with taking photos was creepy.

As an antidote to the odd incident, and the silly budding attraction she'd had for the man, Jackie picked up the telephone receiver in the hall and dialled Adrian's number. He'd be at work now and would only answer if he wasn't busy, but she'd take that chance.

She sighed with relief when his rich voice answered. He wasn't always an easy person to get on with, but she knew where she was with him.

'Adrian, it's Jackie.'

'Hello, sweetheart.'

She took comfort in the ready endearment. Halfway through the conversation, Denise came down the stairs, sitting near the bottom, peering through the banisters. She silently mimicked Jackie's words, pulling a face as she did so. Jackie flicked her hand and mouthed, 'Go away.' But Denise wouldn't budge.

'So you do miss me?' Adrian said, unaware of the sideshow.

'Yes.' Dealing with Scott's skulduggery today had made her realise just how much.

'Then why are you still in Sussex and not in Suffolk?'

She'd explained this several times already.

'You know why. And I want to keep an eye on Denise as she's become a right little madam.'

Denise stuck her tongue out as she ran past her sister and down to the kitchen.

'I do miss you,' Adrian crooned. 'I don't know why you had to leave me alone. Stanley and Iris are your parents, not your children.'

An immense guilt stole over her. She wanted to keep him and her parents happy, yet it seemed there was no compromise.

'Adrian, I don't even have a home to

go back to.'

'Since you don't want to move in with me, I have the solution to that. I saw Yvette earlier. She said she has a spare room and was thinking of looking for a lodger. Why not give her a call? Here's her number.'

Jackie grabbed the ballpoint and wrote the number down on the pad of paper.

Their friend, Yvette — well, more Adrian's friend — had made a kind offer. Yet she knew it wouldn't be like home.

'I have to go now, darling,' Adrian said. 'Please give it some serious thought.'

When he'd hung up, Jackie tore the sheet from the pad and stared at it.

She was twenty-four and grown up now. Using her parents as an excuse to stay at home was just that — an excuse. It was time to cut the apron strings and return to Ipswich.

Unpleasant Surprises

Scott lay on his bed, staring up at the ceiling. The feeling that he was going about this the wrong way wouldn't leave him. As for Jackie spotting him . . . He groaned and turned on his side. What would she be thinking? She clearly hadn't believed the guff about taking photos of Victorian terraces.

He slipped off the bed and went to the window, looking out at the common and beyond, the sea. Dora Perkins — Doreen Parson. It could have been her, if they'd got the name wrong.

His mind wandered to Adrian, picturing him sitting with that superior manner, looking down his nose at everyone. He didn't seem right for Jackie.

During the course of the afternoon tea last week, he'd shown that his appreciation of art was all down to its value. Scott suspected he looked at life in general like that, like nothing had any worth unless it was useful to him in some way.

If he and Jackie ever got married he could imagine her as a trophy on his arm, being shown off. At home she'd be the little woman, all her energies spent on making his life better. It saddened him. There was so much more to her, even if she didn't realise it herself. She was thoughtful, creative, curious. Yet she'd more than likely end up as Adrian's servant. That man lacked imagination, it was clear.

Whereas he had far too much, he concluded. He could only guess at Jackie's reaction had she been privy to his thoughts.

She'd have told him to mind his own business, and quite rightly. He'd completely blown his chances with her. That is, the chances of going on another trip out. That's what he'd meant. Hadn't he?

He returned to the problem of Dora Perkins. He still thought she was too young to be the right person, but then people were always telling him he looked young for twenty-eight. It was only by chance he'd seen the notice in the local paper about her and the tree falling on her house.

He had to face it, she wasn't the right age. He'd been fooling himself in the desperate hope that he'd found her. Where to go from here? Back to the library. He could check the newspapers further back in time and also more of the directories.

She might have moved further away, somewhere not covered by the local directory. Or she might have moved away from the area completely. Then he'd be back to square one.

Two days later, Jackie still hadn't made up her mind whether to tell her parents about catching Scott spying. Mr Grant. She didn't want to be on familiar terms with him any more. A niggle of doubt prevented her. There might be an innocent, or at least, proper reason for what he'd been doing. She had a dim hope that he wasn't some villain.

She'd just reached the hall when she heard uneven steps coming down the stairs from the first floor. A voice was moaning.

'Oh dear, oh dear.'

Jackie went to the foot of the stairs and looked up.

'Are you all right, Mrs Furst? You're late down to breakfast for you.'

She was limping, holding Archie in one hand and clutching the handrail with the other.

'No dear, I'm not all right. My purse has gone missing. It had five pounds in it.'

'Have you searched your room?'

'Top and bottom, every nook and cranny. Not a sausage.'

Archie let out several little yips.

'No, silly boy. I haven't any sausages yet. I swear he knows the word.'

'Come and have your breakfast first. I'll tell my parents what's happened and we'll make a search after you've eaten.'

She accompanied Mrs Furst into the dining-room. Her mother was already there, chatting to the couple who'd arrived on Friday.

'Mum, can I have a word?'

'Excuse me,' she told the couple, then strolled over to the table nearest the door, where the old lady had settled herself.

Mrs Furst explained again what had happened. Scott was on the next table, taking an interest in the conversation.

There were clonking footsteps down the stairs before the door flew open to reveal Denise. Her school tie was squint and her skirt rolled up at the waist to make it shorter.

'I don't want breakfast, Mum. I'm going straight to school.'

Iris held up her hand.

'Before you go rushing off, young lady, have you seen a purse lying about anywhere?'

'A green one,' Mrs Furst clarified.

'No. See you!'

'She's certainly eager to get to school now,' the old lady said. 'It's good to see that after what happened.'

Iris snorted.

'She'll be sorry by morning break when her stomach's rumbling.'

'Let's go over your movements,' Jackie

said. 'See if you can remember something that will give us a clue.'

'And I'll get your usual sausages, egg and tomatoes while you do that.' Iris left the room.

'Well dear, I definitely had it when I went out yesterday. I paid for lunch at the Sea Breezes. I bought an ice-cream further along the row.

'Later, when I took Archie for his afternoon walk, I got a postcard from the Links View gift shop. Yes, that was the last place I got my purse out.'

Jackie held her chin and pondered. It could have been lifted from her handbag on the way, or at dinner. It was often hanging open. The short-term guests were always the most likely suspects.

Glancing at the older couple, a happy pair if ever she'd met one, she decided against it. Besides, they were sitting at the opposite side of the room at dinner, like they were this morning.

The telephone rang in the hall. About to see to it, the noise stopped. Soon after, her father came in to the dining-room.

'Phone call for you, Mr Grant,' he said. Scott looked around in surprise.

'For me? OK, thanks.' He left the table, frowning.

Mrs Furst disturbed Jackie's concentration.

'What do you think, dear?'

'About the purse? I think you should go to Links View to see if they've found it. You may simply have dropped it in the shop.'

'Or on the way back. In which case, I'll never find it, as you can be sure some scallywag will have had it.'

Iris returned with the cooked breakfast.

'Here you are, Mrs Furst. And Stanley's just bringing your tea.'

'Lovely. You're so kind.'

Scott followed Stanley in, all the way to Mrs Furst's table.

'Could I have a word? That was my agent on the phone. She's got me an exhibition in London, short notice. Just a small one, in July, but I need to get back today to make preparations. I hope you don't mind. I'll pay until the end of the period I booked.'

'I won't hear of it,' Iris said. 'But I do hope you'll come back to us at some point.' She smiled encouragingly.

Stanley nodded in agreement.

What were her parents up to? They shouldn't be letting him off paying. What's more, it was a little too convenient, given recent events. Her catching him spying, Mrs Furst's purse going missing. She could hardly say this here, though.

Beneath the suspicion, a tiny bit of her was disappointed. He was the most interesting person she'd met in ages. She brushed the thought aside. It had no place here any more.

'That is kind of you,' Scott said, 'and yes, I should like to return at some point.'

The Watts entered the dining-room, invariably the last to come down to breakfast.

'My, there's quite a crowd gathered in here,' Rita said.

'Mrs Furst has lost her purse,' Jackie

explained. 'If you could look out for it, it would be appreciated.'

'Poor you, Mrs Furst.' Rita stroked her arm and made a fuss of her.

'Yes, jolly bad luck,' Raymond agreed.

'And Mr Grant is leaving us to mount an exhibition in London,' Iris added, as proud as if he'd been her own son.

'How exciting!' Rita clapped her hands. 'Where exactly? Raymond and I would love to pay a visit.'

'I haven't the address on me. Tell you what, I'll send details in the post.'

'What exactly will you be showing?' Raymond asked.

'I've yet to decide. Now, if you'll excuse me, I need to pack.'

When he left the room, the Watts sat down. Iris left her daughter to take their order.

'It's all very cloak and dagger, isn't it?' Rita said. 'You think he'd remember the venue so he could tell people about it.'

'I guess he's excited and the details have gone out of his head,' Jackie said.

'Or he's not really an artist at all. I

have wondered. It's not like he's done much sketching. Maybe he's a fantasist, like Billy Liar.'

Mrs Watt could be closer to the truth than she realised, Jackie thought.

'Either way, he's leaving us so we don't need to worry about it.'

It was as much a reply to herself as to Mrs Watt.

After giving the order to her parents she came back up to her bedroom on the ground floor, to get ready for her shift at the funfair. On the mat she found a letter addressed to her. The handwriting was Adrian's. It would be something to read during her break.

'Goodbye, Mr Grant,' she mouthed as she left the house and didn't look back.

999!

Jackie was grateful to be working at the funfair that day, thinking the ghost train would distract her. Try as she might, the knowledge that Scott was leaving Mare Vista wouldn't go away. If only she could have got to the bottom of what he'd been up to. Clearly he'd obtained whatever he'd come for and was heading back to wherever he'd hailed from. Maybe not London at all.

A family stopped by, looking at the carriages of the ghost train.

'Come inside for a spooky ride,' she said in a ghostly voice, trying to tempt them in. She'd made up a few phrases to stir the customers' interest. It was better than standing around doing nothing, as she'd seen the guy on the Waltzer do.

It did the trick and soon she was setting two cars off around the track.

There was a lull after quarter to twelve, with people going for lunch. Balanced on a stool she faced the entrance, looking for the arrival of potential clients. She was pleasantly surprised to see Gary walk in. A chat with him would pass some of the time.

He did a sweep of the area. Spotting her, he headed over.

'Hey, what's the buzz?' he said as he got closer.

'Hi, Gary.'

'Val told us about your sister. She OK now?'

'Yeah. The school sorted it out and she's made some friends.'

'Neat. Good for her.'

There was an awkward moment of silence that Jackie filled.

'How are you, then?'

'It's my day off so I'm chilling out. Thought I'd take a walk since it was such a nice day.'

She half hoped he'd suggest meeting up after work. She could do with something to look forward to. Especially as she had a bombshell to drop when she got home. It had been two days since her decision to go back to Ipswich and she still hadn't told her parents. She'd need to tell her boss here, too.

Adrian wouldn't be happy about her hanging out with Gary, but it might be the last time, so what was the harm? It would give her an opportunity to tell him she was leaving.

'It is a lovely day. Wish I wasn't cooped up in here. Still, I'll be out at four.' She looked at her watch.

She hoped that might encourage Gary to suggest meeting up.

'I was wondering . . . ' Here we go, she thought. '. . . if, um, Val worked nearby.'

Val? She wanted to laugh. It was like he was going to suggest meeting up but had chickened out.

'She works on the Merry Mixer, the other side of the Waltzer.'

'Oh, yeah, of course. I'll pop round there and say hello, too. I'll, er, see ya around then.'

'Yeah. Sure.'

He sauntered off, lifting a hand.

She watched him as he passed the mirror maze and rifle range. Oh, well, looked like she'd be in for the evening. It was just as well. She was putting off the inevitable. The longer she left it, the worse it would be.

An hour or so later she was sent off for lunch. She took her sandwich and yoghurt to the grass by the Oyster Pond, where she found Val already finishing up her lunch.

'How's your morning been?' Val asked. 'It's been pretty boring round my side.'

'Yeah, same with the ghost train. Apart from Gary turning up for a brief natter.'

'Gary?'

'It's his day off and he was taking a walk.' Val laughed.

'Doesn't sound like Gary. He likes listening to his music and playing his bass guitar when he's not at work.'

'He asked where you were and said he'd pop round and say hello.'

Val stuck her bottom lip out.

'I didn't see him. Maybe it was an excuse to talk to you and he had no intention of coming to see me.'

'I did wonder if he'd come to ask me

out but bottled it.'

'There you go, then.' Val got up, rubbing the grass off her loons and cheesecloth top.

'My lunchtime's over so I'd better get back to the grindstone. You walking back after the shift?'

'Yep.' The dread slithered across her insides once more. She'd tell Val her plans on the way home. Apart from her family, she was the person she'd most miss in Littlehampton.

'You all right? You've gone all serious,' Val said.

'Yeah, I'll be OK. Got something to tell you on our way back.'

'That sounds ominous. Right, see ya later.'

Jackie took the letter from Adrian out of her bag and started reading it. When she'd finished, she spent the rest of her lunch break forming the right words for her parents. It didn't matter how she put it to herself, she knew they were going to be upset.

'So, Scott was photographing the woman from the end house, next to the junior school,' Val said, as the pair of them walked back to Jackie's that afternoon.

'That's right.' Jackie nodded. 'It's what it looked like, anyway. He said he was taking pictures of the interesting Victorian architecture, but . . . '

'You're not convinced.'

'No.'

Jackie didn't know why she was going over this again now, maybe to get some insight that would let Scott off the hook. Even now, she'd rather not think badly of him.

'That would be Dora Perkins,' Val said. 'A tree fell on to the back of the house recently, that's why there's scaffolding up.'

'Could he be a reporter trying to find out what really happened? What if it was . . . ' She ran out of ideas.

'An old tree fell over. It's hardly a crime.'

138

Jackie breathed in deeply before letting it out in a long sigh.

'I don't know, then.' She stopped, twisting towards Val. 'Hang on. Did you say Dora Perkins?'

'Yes. What of it?'

'It's just, that morning, he asked me if I knew anyone by the name of Doreen Parson. She was a friend of his mother's, apparently.'

Val pulled a face.

'They're similar names, I'll give you that, but not so much that you'd mix them up. And Dora's far too young to be a friend of his mother's, surely.'

'Especially as Scott said his mother had been dead some years.'

'It's a mystery, that's for certain. Or it was a crime about to be committed. But why alert you to it by asking about someone with a similar name?'

'Oh, I don't know.'

'Come on, better get a move on.'

They crossed the road from the Oyster Pond to The Nelson.

'Anyway,' Val went on, 'he's leaving

for this 'exhibition', or whatever it really is, so you can forget him. To be honest, I always thought he was a bit weird.'

Jackie looked sidelong at her friend and laughed.

'That's not what you said when you first met him.'

'Yeah, well, it's what I'm saying now.'

This was the time to tell Val of her imminent departure.

'Change of subject . . . Have you been out with Stuart again?' Trust her to bottle out.

'Only as a friend.' Val seemed a bit put out.

Perhaps she was hoping to go out with him properly and he wasn't interested?

'I've known Stuart and Gary a long time. They used to live on Beaconsfield Road. Are you actually interested in Gary?' It was said a little critically, as if she was accusing Jackie of stringing him along.

Right, this was the moment.

'It's irrelevant now. I'm going back to Ipswich.'

Val spun around. 'What?'

Jackie pulled Adrian's letter out of her bag and handed it to her friend. She scanned the lines, shaking her head all the while.

'So he's organised your lodgings and a job for you at his firm.'

'I'll have to give in my notice at my old firm. I was only on a sabbatical for the summer.'

'Goodness, your ex-boyfriend is thorough. Or is he your boyfriend again now?'

'I'll have to decide that when I go back. The whole relationship's been a bit confused since I got here. We were on a break, but I still kind of felt he was my boyfriend.'

Val handed her the letter back.

'Maybe that's because you didn't want to split up in the first place.'

Jackie wondered that. Then why had she been so keen to move down to Littlehampton? She could tell herself over and over that it was to make sure her parents were OK. The fact was, they were coping

141

well and the business was thriving.

'You're probably right, Val.'

They'd reached Mare Vista by this time. Jackie dawdled at the bottom of the steps.

'What do your parents think about it?'

She groaned.

'I haven't told them yet. I'm not looking forward to it. It'd be one thing if I was simply getting my own place, but being so far from them as well . . . It'll be very strange.'

'People do it all the time. I'd move out of my parents' house if I could afford it. But until I settle on a proper job it's a pipe dream. Will I see you tomorrow, or are you going immediately?'

'No, not immediately. So yes, I'll see you tomorrow.'

Val headed away. What fun it would have been if they could have moved in somewhere together as flat mates. It would never be, and no doubt they'd lose touch eventually. Such a shame. All her close friends from school had moved away. Her life had been dominated by her relationship with Adrian since she was seventeen, so she'd never made any new friends, not close ones.

In the hall she looked up the stairs to the first floor, then down the stairs to the basement. All was quiet. Her parents had said they'd be going out in the afternoon to do some food shopping, so they were likely still out. Denise was probably dawdling with her new friends.

She looked at the phone, biting the edge of her lip, before picking it up and dialling Adrian's number.

'Carter and Hibbard Ltd, Adrian Carter speaking.'

'Hello, Adrian, it's Jackie.'

'Hello, sweetheart. I'll have to be quick, I've got a meeting in ten minutes.'

'I'll have to be quick, too. I received your letter this morning and I thought you'd like to know that I've decided I will come back.'

'That's wonderful, darling. I knew you'd see sense. And I hope you agree it would be a good idea for you to work for me instead of returning to your old job.'

'I suppose so, but . . .'

'Good. Now when are you travelling up?'

The stress of it all made her feel light-headed.

'Give me a chance. I haven't even told my parents yet. And I might have to give some notice at work.'

'Not for casual labour, surely. Yvette can take you in straight away.'

Take her in, like she was a waif and stray? Not the best way for him to put it.

'Give me time to breathe, Adrian. It's a big step. I'll be back in the next week or so, two at the most.'

'I'm so looking forward to having you back.' Another unfortunate phrase, as if he'd let her go in the first place.

'Let's take it slowly, Adrian, please. I need to settle in, at my new home and at the new job.'

'Don't you worry about that. I'm sure you'll do fine. I'll look after everything.'

That's what she was afraid of, after having so much freedom these last months. She'd have to lay down a few

144

ground rules when she got back.

'We'll talk about it when I return. Got to go. I can hear my parents coming in the back.'

'See you soon, sweetheart.'

'Yes, soon.'

Down the stairs she found Stanley and Iris putting shopping bags on the table.

'I'll help you put stuff away,' Jackie told them.

'Thanks, love,' Stanley said. 'By the way, Mrs Furst went along to Links View, but they hadn't seen her purse.'

'What a shame. I'm not sure what else anyone can do. It's hardly a police matter.'

'The other news is that we have new guests arriving at the weekend,' Iris said. 'I'll put them in Scott's room since it's free. It's got the better view.'

Scott's room, like he'd been there long enough to claim ownership. It felt rather odd to think he wasn't here any more. He's gone and he's history! And soon she'd be gone too.

'Mum, Dad, I have some news.'

'Have you got yourself a proper job?' Iris asked. 'A nice office job, like your last one?'

'In a way. It's just that it's . . .'

Denise barged into the kitchen, throwing her tote bag on to a kitchen chair.

'Can't stop. I'm doing my homework at Gillian's house and Ruth's coming over so I won't be back till dinner.'

'And where does she live?' Iris asked, rubbing her side.

'You all right, Mum?' Denise asked.

'Yes. Just indigestion again.' She sat down and breathed slowly.

'Write the address here, just in case.' Jackie pushed the note pad and pen that her parents used for shopping lists towards her sister.

'In case of what?'

'In case we need to get hold of you.'

Denise did as she was asked and rushed off to get changed.

'You were telling us about a new job you have,' Stanley prompted.

'That's part of it. The other part's . . .'

A sudden howl came from her mother,

146

who grabbed at her right side. Jackie and Stanley rushed to her.

'Whatever's wrong, Iris?'

'Mum?'

The howl became a long moan.

'It really hurts. And I feel sick.'

'Jackie, call an ambulance,' Stanley ordered. She rushed off upstairs. 'I told you to see a doctor,' she heard her father add.

Jackie remembered the stab of pain her mother had suffered when they'd found out about Denise missing school. Dad had said then it wasn't the first time. By the time Jackie picked the receiver up she could hardly get the words out, so overpowering was the dread. She was almost crying.

'Ambulance, please!' she said.

Change of Plan

'I don't want to go to school today.' Denise was crying as Jackie came rushing down to the kitchen, having just taken three orders from breakfast.

She didn't have time for this now.

'Mum's had the operation and she's come through it well. They say it looks like it's going to be fine.'

'That's not the same as they're sure it will be. Dad said if they'd waited any longer to remove her appendix it might have burst. Then who knows what might have happened?'

Jackie put her arms round her sister. What on earth had possessed her father to say that to Denise when he'd returned home last night? Clearly not thinking straight after all the panic.

'But it didn't burst and now it's been removed.'

'I still don't want to go to school. I want to come to the hospital with you and visit Mum.'

There was no point in arguing.

'In that case, why don't you don a pinny and give me a hand? I could do with someone to serve while I cook the breakfasts. Cleaning needs to be done, plus getting a room ready for guests arriving tomorrow, if you could help me with that. I don't think Dad's going to be up to it today.'

Stanley had arrived back late last night, having followed the ambulance to Worthing Hospital earlier that day. He'd got up earlier but had only slept a couple of hours and had looked terrible. She'd sent him back to bed for the morning.

Denise cheered up and nodded.

'I'd rather do that, keep busy. And it would please Mum, too, us all mucking in.'

She was a good little worker when she put her mind to it.

'First of all Mrs Furst would like a pot of tea and the other guests a pot of coffee. I'll start on the sausages.'

They set to work, Jackie absorbed completing the different meals, Denise carrying the various plates, pots and jugs up, then bringing used ones down.

'I'd better ring the school soon,' Jackie said when they'd finished all the orders. 'And I'll have to ring the manager at the funfair, too. He's not going to be happy with me, especially after disappearing when I went up to Ipswich.'

'Sorry about that.' Denise looked away, her mouth down at the corners.

Jackie hugged her sister once more.

'There's no need to be. It all worked out fine.'

'I'm glad you didn't stay behind in Ipswich. It wouldn't be like a complete family without you here.'

Jackie felt awkward. How would Denise take the news that she'd have to break to her eventually? Not now though. Which reminded her — she needed to ring Adrian, too. He wouldn't be happy, but he'd understand. That one could wait till later.

'I'll make those calls, then we can set about finishing up here and tidying upstairs as the guests leave.'

'OK. I'll go and see how they're get-ting on.'

Jackie removed her apron.

'Right, phone calls.'

* * *

Jackie had driven her dad and Denise to Worthing Hospital after lunch, arriving in the ward just after two o'clock, when visiting for the afternoon began.

Denise was first by her bedside, taking her hand where it lay on top of the cover.

'How are you, Mum?' Iris managed a tiny smile.

'In pain, but at least I know this one will go away as I heal.'

Iris's face went serious and she attempted to sit up. Jackie restrained her.

'Don't do that, Mum, you'll do your-self a mischief.'

'But the guests, what did you do for dinner?'

'I got them all fish and chips in,' Jackie said, 'which they were more than happy with. Mrs Furst and the Watts send their best wishes, by the way.'

Jackie realised Scott would have been on that list, had he not left. Stop thinking about him!

'Thank you for holding the fort.'

'And Denise helped me with breakfast.' Jackie put her arm around her sister's shoulders. 'She did a really good job of the serving while I cooked.'

'There's a good girl.' Iris patted her younger daughter's hand.

'I'll help with dinner, too, this evening,' she said eagerly. 'Dad's gonna do his coq au vin and Jackie and I are going to make a lemon meringue pie.'

'Sounds lovely. The doctor said I'll have to be in a few days. How will you cope? I could discharge myself.'

'You'll do no such thing.' Stanley leaned over her, looking a mixture of cross and concerned, his eyebrows meeting in the middle. 'You'll take as long as you need to get better, you hear? We'll cope all right.'

'Of course we will,' Jackie reassured her.

An hour later, as they were leaving, they were waylaid by the white-coated doctor.

'Mrs Harris is doing very well,' he told them, 'but she'll be in hospital for ten days. After that she'll need to recover at home for several weeks. I believe you run a guest house?'

'That's right,' Stanley said.

'She mustn't do housework or anything that puts a strain on her abdomen.'

'Will she get back to normal?' Denise sounded like a distressed six-year-old, reminding Jackie that she hadn't quite grown up yet.

'Without a doubt.' The doctor treated her to a wide grin. 'Just so long as she rests and heals.'

'Don't worry, doctor, she won't have to lift a finger,' Jackie said. Even if it did mean adding several weeks to her departure date.

Outside the hospital building, on the way to the car, Stanley came to an abrupt halt.

'What's up, Dad?' Denise asked.

Stanley lowered his head. His shoulders started shaking and Jackie realised he had tears rolling down his cheeks.

'Oh, Dad.'

'I'm so glad both my girls are here.' He placed his arms round their shoulders. 'I don't know what I would have done without you. I thought I was going to lose your mum.'

The girls looked helplessly on as their father sobbed. Jackie realised her father wasn't going to cope with the guesthouse, taking care of Mum and looking after Denise on his own. Ten days, six weeks or whatever the duration, she'd be putting her departure on hold for as long as it took.

* * *

Iris had been home four days now. She'd spent the first two days tucked up in bed, but on the third had announced that she couldn't bear to be away from everyone and was going to sit on the settee, feet up, with a good book. At least then she could see people and join in conversations.

Jackie was currently getting things prepared ahead of time for dinner.

Iris lifted her head and peered towards the kitchen area.

'Are you making chocolate mousse?'

Jackie gave her the kind of look Mum herself was fond of giving when a little peeved.

'What did Dad tell you about not getting involved? Leave the decisions to us.'

Iris put her book down.

'It's sensible, I know that, but I've never been one for sitting around.'

'I know, Mum. But you don't want to go injuring yourself and then have to spend even longer recuperating.'

'I guess not.'

'If you must know, I am making chocolate mousse. I'm using your recipe.'

'I'm sure you'll do wonderfully.' Iris looked through the window. 'Such a nice day, too. I could do with a walk outside, not just round and round the settee for exercise.'

'Let's see how you get on and maybe in a couple of days you can do a circuit of the garden.'

'I might even sit out there for a little while. I'm sure the sun would do me good. Goodness, it'll be July tomorrow. Where's the time gone?'

Jackie had been thinking the same. It had been two weeks since she'd resigned from the funfair. Two weeks since she'd told Adrian she wouldn't be back yet. He'd been amazingly understanding, yet she felt his patience could only last so long. She rubbed her temples with her fingers.

'You got a headache?' Iris asked.

'No. Well, just a little. It's the heat.' She didn't want to admit that trying to please all of the people all of the time was becoming a burden.

'By the way, I suddenly remembered this morning. Just before I went into hospital you said something about a new job.'

Dad had asked about this the day after Mum had gone into hospital. She gave

156

her the same reply.

'No, It was more that there was a possible job I was looking at. That's all. I'll look again after you're well.'

The phone rang from the hall.

'I'd better get that,' Jackie said. 'Might be more bookings.' She headed upstairs.

Currently they had all six available rooms booked until next week, but they had several gaps over the course of the summer.

'Littlehampton 4528.'

'It's me.'

Adrian. It was nice having a break to hear his voice.

'Hello. You've got me mid mousse making.'

'Perhaps you could make me one when you return to Ipswich. I've always liked a good homemade mousse. We'll have dinner a deux at mine. You're such a good cook.

I'll provide the wine.'

'Perhaps I will.' This was more the Adrian she'd fallen in love with.

'Of course, you'll have to come back

for that to happen. Any idea when that will be?' It was said light-heartedly, but it was pressure she didn't need nonetheless.

'Mum's not long out of hospital. She's banned from working for several weeks. At least six.'

'Six weeks? But that'll be the middle of August. Summer will be nearly over.'

'Apart from Mum's condition, Dad's been knocked for six. He can't do both their jobs. Denise helps where she can but she's got school.'

'She'll be on summer holiday soon,' Adrian pointed out. 'And who are you keeping the business going for? A batty old woman and a dotty middle-aged couple. Not to mention that odd artist chap whom no-one had actually heard of.'

She hadn't mentioned anything about his departure to Adrian, mainly because she hadn't wanted him crowing over the incident as if he'd won a victory.

'It's our busiest time and we've had other people staying. And you shouldn't knock the long term guests as they're guaranteed money.'

'Don't know what possessed your parents to up sticks and open such a place at their time of life.'

'Their time of life? They're only in their early fifties. Where exactly is this conversation getting us?'

'I resent the fact they took you away from me. I do miss you.'

Her heart softened, which didn't help what she had to do.

'Look, Adrian, I can't give you a date for my return. It wouldn't be fair on you, and it certainly wouldn't be fair on my family.'

'Yvette will have to let the room to someone else. She can't wait indefinitely.'

'So be it.' Living in the house of someone she didn't know well, confined to one room and the kitchen, had never appealed to her.

'If that's the — the case, maybe we should — should split up once and for all,' Adrian announced.

By the faltering way he said it, she

knew he was using it as a way to encourage her to give in. She'd play him at his own game.

'If you think that's for the best, Adrian.'

'I, um, well, no, it's not for the best.'

Stanley appeared at the top of the stairs, hovering nearby.

She made her voice quieter.

'Or, you could move closer to me. You're an accountant. You could move anywhere.'

'I can't talk about it now,' he said brusquely. 'I'm busy.'

'Me, too. And I think Dad might want the phone. Speak to you later.'

She hung up. Calling his bluff had been an excellent idea, even though she'd done it in the heat of the moment.

'Was that Adrian?' Stanley asked, irritated.

'Yes, it was,' she answered shortly. She regretted matching her father's tone. They were all under pressure.

'He doesn't give up, does he?'

'Look, I know you've hoped to keep me apart from him, but you know what they say about absence and hearts growing fonder.'

He grunted.

'Never did think he was right for you.'

She handed him the phone receiver.

'Here, it's all yours.'

'That's not what I'm here for. I forgot to tell you before I went out. While you were cleaning upstairs, Scott Grant rang to ask if he could return tomorrow. It so happens his room will be free, which is handy.'

'His room' again, as if he owned it!

'Didn't we have an enquiry about it?'

'That fell through earlier this morning. It'll be good to have him back.'

It was on the tip of her tongue to tell her dad about the incident in Beaconsfield Road, but something stopped her. Dad had been happier the last couple of days. She didn't want to spoil that.

She'd deal with him herself.

A Word of Caution

'Here we are then.' Stanley ushered Scott into the hall as Jackie came down the stairs from the first floor. 'Look who's arrived.'

She guessed she was supposed to welcome him enthusiastically from Dad's announcement, but she couldn't go that far.

'Welcome back to Mare Vista,' she said with a half smile, hoping that exhibited the right amount of professionalism.

'I was very sorry to hear about your mother,' Scott said. 'What a shock for you all.'

'It was, rather. So what happened to this exhibition?'

Her father had already told her Scott's excuse, but she wanted to hear it from him.

'I decided to defer it until August, when hopefully I can add a few more paintings. I need to see to some unfinished business first.' He seemed to close up after the last sentence.

'Help him up to the room, would you, Jacqueline?' Stanley said.

'I'll take the heavier bags if you take these.' Scott pointed to some large, thin rectangles, three of them in all, about two feet by three feet.

They had to make two trips up, Scott taking one of the rectangles on his last journey. He set it against the wall with the other two.

'What are they?' Jackie asked.

'Paintings I need to finish. Would you like to see them?'

'Yes, I would.' Let's see how good a painter he is, she thought.

He carefully unwrapped the first one, folding the plastic sheeting and brown paper carefully. No doubt he'd need to transport them back again.

Her mouth fell open when she saw the first one. It was unmistakably her, standing on the walls of Arundel Castle. Even unfinished it was good.

'Wow, that's skilful.' She took a closer look.

'Thank you. It's from one of the photos I took. I was wondering . . . ' He looked unsure.

'Wondering what?'

'If you might sit for me, so I can get your face right.'

Would there be any harm in it? She thought for a while.

'When I have some time off, yes. What are the other two?'

He unwrapped them to reveal the River Arun from Pier Road, and the beach from the pier.

'They're good, too. They've got a hint of Monet about them, but not so impressionist.'

He laughed.

'I should be as gifted as him!'

'But you are gifted all the same.' She didn't want to go over the top. After all, she still didn't know what he'd been up to when he was here before. 'I'll leave you to unpack and see you at dinner.'

She left the room, relieved to get away from him. It would be so easy to get pulled back in by his apparent charm. Not a second time, no.

* * *

That evening Jackie took her mum a cup of tea to where she was tucked up on the sofa, half watching the Saturday Film on TV.

'You didn't say much about Scott's arrival,' Iris said.

'What's to tell? He's back.' Jackie shrugged. She was determined they would be her only words on the matter, but her mother had other ideas.

'Dad said Scott told him he's brought some paintings to finish. I wonder what they are.'

Jackie gave in and sat on the armchair next to the sofa.

'They're of the Arun and the beach. And, er, one of me on the battlements at Arundel Castle.'

'How lovely! You might find yourself in that exhibition.'

'On display in London? I shouldn't

165

think so. He's got to finish it yet and wants me to sit for him. Do you think I should?'

Mum leaned forward.

'Of course you should. It's a pity you didn't go to college. You had a talent. You don't seem to draw at all now.'

Jackie thought about all the half-filled art books she had on the shelves in her room. There were sketches, drawings with pastel and coloured pencils, and a large book with paintings. She still had her art folder from A-Level, filled with all sorts of creations.

'If nothing else, it would be a nice hobby. You don't seem to have any of those now. You used to go to hockey club and sing in the choral society. Until Adrian started taking up all your time.'

Jackie got up from the seat.

'That's what happens when you grow up, Mum.'

Iris took hold of her hand.

'Don't be cross. I realise my illness has made life difficult for you and that it's prevented you going back to Ipswich.'

'Why do you say that?'

'Adrian rang yesterday looking for you when you were out. Dad answered it. Adrian got cross about you being 'stuck' with helping at the guesthouse. He explained that you'd been about to leave and that we'd ruined your plans for your new job and the flat you were going to rent. He upset Dad.'

Trust Adrian to open his mouth. She'd told him she'd deal with it all, but no, he had to interfere.

'I'm sorry he upset you both. I was going to tell you my plans just as you had the pains. I've put them on hold and wouldn't give him a date. He had no right to tell Dad that.'

Mum squeezed her hand a little more.

'I remember you saying something about a job. If you really feel you need to go, we'll manage. We can always reduce the number of visitors.'

'You'll do no such thing. The new job was only at Adrian's firm, doing what I'd done in my old job.'

She wasn't even sure why she'd agreed

to it now, given that her old firm would have taken her back after the summer when the temp had gone.

'As for the so-called flat, it was a room in the house of one of Adrian's friends. He really is the giddy limit!'

'As long as you're sure.'

Jackie took both her mum's hands in hers.

'Yes, I am, Mum. Absolutely sure.'

There was a firm knock on the front door upstairs.

'Who's that now?' Iris said.

'Perhaps one of the guests has locked themselves out.' She took off her apron and headed to the ground floor.

Through the frosted glass she could see it was Val. She would have finished her shift at the funfair now. Jackie rushed to the door, glad to see her friend. She'd been afraid they might lose contact now they weren't working together.

'Hi, Val. Lovely to see you.'

Her friend held out a large bunch of yellow roses.

'I thought I'd come round to see how

your mum is, and bring her these.'

'Come in. Can you spare a few minutes to say hello? She likes having visitors.'

'Of course. I'm meeting Gary, Stuart and a couple of other girls who were at the party, but not till eight-thirty.'

Jackie had a moment of regret that she wasn't invited. She could do with getting out. She'd been too tired most evenings to think of ringing Val.

'Come down.'

'Well, well, you're a sight for sore eyes,' Iris said, spotting Val on the stairs.

'I've brought some flowers, Mrs Harris, to cheer you up.' She handed them over.

'They're beautiful, dear, thank you.'

Jackie took them to put into water as her father came down with the mop bucket.

'That's all clean for tomorrow now. Oh hello, Val. It's nice to see you. Are you and Jackie going out somewhere nice?'

'She's just called round with flowers, Dad.' Jackie felt embarrassed in case Val thought it was a hint.

'I'd love Jackie to come if she can. I thought she'd be tied up with dinner and what not.'

'Dinner's at six-thirty here, so we're usually done now,' Stanley said.

'You're quite welcome to come,' Val said. 'We're only going to the high street for a Chinese.'

'I haven't started on the washing up yet.'

'Oh, go on with you.' Her father came and undid her apron. 'It won't take me long. And Denise can come and do the drying.'

'Are you sure?'

'Go on, go and get changed,' Iris said.

Jackie looked at Val who looked pleased, so that was something. She hurried up to her bedroom, threw on a mini dress and grabbed her platform sandals.

Out in the hall she heard Denise from her bedroom.

'But I'm listening to Radio Luxembourg.'

'Come on. You've been out all day with your friends. Let your sister have an evening off.'

'Oh, all right.'

How quickly things got back to normal.

Jackie called down the stairs.

'I'm ready. Bye, Mum.'

When she and Val got outside, Jackie took a large gulp of air.

'It's good to be out, and not just to do the shopping or pick up a guest.'

'I bet. Your mum told me that Scott's returned to the guest house.'

They rounded the corner and made their way into town.

Jackie frowned.

'You didn't say anything about what I told you, did you?'

'Of course not. I could tell she didn't know about it. What are you going to do? He might be here to cause more mischief.'

'I don't know if he was causing mischief in the first place. At least I discovered he can actually paint. He brought three paintings with him. They look good, even though they're not finished.' She didn't like to admit that one of them was of her.

'He still might be some kind of con merchant. Perhaps he does forgeries.'

Jackie screwed up her face.

'What? And I thought I had a vivid imagination.'

'Just be careful, that's all.'

'I will, don't worry.'

★ ★ ★

When the group walked Jackie to her home that night, there was still a hint of light in the west.

Val did her jacket up, and called to the others.

'I'm just having a word with Jackie. If you dawdle ahead I'll catch up.'

'What's up?' Jackie said.

Val waited until the group were out of earshot.

'I've been thinking about Scott Grant. Perhaps you should have a word with the police. You never know, you might prevent a crime.'

'I don't want to go upsetting things if

it wasn't what it looked like. He's a paying guest, after all. I might just face him with what I suspect, see what he says.'

'It's up to you. At least you'll be out of here soon.'

'Not sure when.' Jackie laughed.

'I haven't told anyone else yet, but I've applied for a full time job in an office in Worthing. There are prospects of promotion and what not. I thought, you're moving on, why don't I? Then I could earn enough money to get a rental, maybe.'

'That sounds great, Val.' Jackie hugged her.

'The job's not mine yet, but the interview went well.'

'Well, good luck to you.'

'Thanks. You know, I've got a feeling it's going to be my year.'

Jackie was thrilled for her, though she wished she felt so positive about her own future.

'Talk of the devil. There's Scott now. He must have been out for one of those evening walks he's so fond of.' Jackie indicated where he was crossing the side road that Gary and the others had already crossed, going in the opposite direction.

'Be careful,' Val said. 'I'd better catch the others up. See ya.' She ran down the pavement. Scott looked round at her as she flew past him.

When he spotted Jackie he speeded up. This could be the time to tackle him, out of the house so out of earshot of others. She tried to work out how to word it so it didn't sound like an accusation, though it would be.

As Scott got near enough to greet her, she launched into her speech.

'Now you're here alone, I want to ask you about why you were spying on Dora Perkins.'

'Honestly, it's not what it looked like.'

'Then what . . .'

Jackie didn't get to finish the sentence before there was a roaring of an unseen, speeding car, followed by the squeal of tyres and a scream.

'Oh my gosh, Val!' Jackie cried. She ran towards the side road, followed by Scott. She could see Stuart, Gary and the others running from the other side of the pavement. When they reached the road a car had stopped, slightly sideways, near the junction.

Lying on the road, unmoving, was Val.

The Story is Out

Jackie walked into Worthing Hospital the next afternoon in a state of nerves. It hadn't been long since the last time she was here, visiting Mum. After a sleepless night, she'd had a phone call from Val's mother to say she'd been in surgery and was stable. Whatever that meant. She wanted to see Val for herself.

Gary had rung her later to say he was driving in and offered her a lift, for which she'd been grateful. He'd been quiet in the car, no doubt as shaken about the situation as she was.

After dropping her off at the entrance, Gary went to park.

Entering the ward, Jackie spotted Val's mum sitting next to the furthest bed. Val was on her back, eyes closed. There were scrapes and bruises on her face, which was swollen. Jackie could hardly bear to look.

'Hello, love, thanks for coming. Val's still asleep but I'm sure she'll appreciate another friendly face when she wakes up.'

'How long have you been here?' Jackie asked.

'Since last night. Her dad and I were in a waiting room for most of the night, then came in here when they brought Valerie out of theatre. She's still groggy from the anaesthetic.'

'Goodness, you must be tired.'

'We'll go home when visiting time is over. They don't really like you staying outside of the hours, but we insisted.'

'You said she's broken her leg and has fractured ribs.'

'Yes. And they found the driver was over the limit. I hope they throw the book at them!' She took out her hankie and wiped the tears from her cheeks.

'I think they might have been going too fast as well. We heard a speeding car just moments before.'

'Yes, that's what the police are thinking, too.'

'Apart from the broken bones, is she — OK?'

'They think so, but time will tell.'

'Are you talking about me behind my back?' came a slow, muffled voice.

'Valerie!' Mrs Matthews stood and leaned over her daughter.

'Hello, Mum. What am I doing here?'

Mrs Matthews looked at Jackie before replying.

'You were run over by a car, love. Don't you remember?'

There was a pause as Val closed her eyes.

'I remember saying cheerio to Jackie ...Then ...No. I don't recall what happened after that.'

'Jackie's here, too.'

'I know.' Her eyelids fluttered, then her eyes opened wide. 'What day is it? What about work?'

Jackie got closer to the bed.

'I rang the funfair, the Blue Sea and the Nelson and explained what happened.'

'Thank you for doing that,' Mrs Matthews said. 'You're a true friend to Valerie.'

Jackie spotted the long blond hair of Gary as he sloped through the ward.

'Oh, look, another visitor.' Val's mum seemed pleased.

'Watcha,' Gary lifted his hand in greeting but he looked in pain himself. 'I'm glad to see you're awake. How are you feeling?'

'Like I've been run over.' She tried a small laugh that turned into a wince.

Mrs Matthews stroked her brow.

'I wouldn't try that for a while. You need to keep still for now.'

'Easier said than done.'

'I'll go and see where your dad's got to. They're not very happy about more than two visitors at a time.'

Jackie sat on the chair while Gary brought another one round to sit next to her.

'Stuart's popping over soon,' he said.

'That's nice.' Val tried a smile, though it emphasised the swelling. 'Any idea how long I'll be out of action? Did Mum say anything before I woke up?'

'No, she didn't,' Jackie said. 'Think

it'll be a few weeks, though.'

'At the very least,' Gary added.

'You've broken a leg and some ribs.'

Val peered up at her suspended leg.

'Hmm. Don't suppose the funfair, café or pub'll keep the jobs open for me, being casual. There'll be plenty of students to hire now they've broken up.'

'You never know,' Gary said. 'Or maybe it'd be an opportunity to get a more permanent job.'

'You sound like my mum.'

'Sorry.' He looked down at his hands.

'Oh, I've just remembered the job I applied for in Worthing.' She groaned. 'Even if I get it, I won't be able to go.'

Gary looked confused. 'What job's this?'

'Office job,' Jackie told him. 'You'll just have to wait and see, Val.'

'So much for it being my year.'

'Talk to me about something other than jobs or accidents,' Val said. 'Take my mind off it.'

'I bought the latest Jethro Tull album a few days ago,' Gary offered. 'Yeah, that's better.'

A conversation on music ensued, mainly between the other two, and Val seemed a tiny bit more cheerful.

Jackie's mind wandered to Scott. She hadn't had the opportunity to get back to the interrupted conversation about Dora Perkins since Val's accident. She'd have to find a time and a place, as she wasn't going to be satisfied until she heard his explanation.

⋆ ⋆ ⋆

Two days had gone by, and still Scott hadn't had a chance to complete his conversation with Jackie. He'd been out a lot and couldn't talk to her at meal times in front of the others.

He was the last to leave the dining-room that evening, lingering as he was over his trifle and coffee. He'd thought about starting the conversation several times, but knew her family would be in to clear and clean tables. There was no point having half a discussion.

Jackie started sweeping the floor, which they didn't normally do when guests were eating. She was clearly dropping a hint that he should hurry up. An idea came to him. Should he? He decided he had nothing to lose.

'I was wondering . . .' he called over.

She looked up.

'After you've finished what you've got to do this evening, would you come for a drink at the Nelson?'

She hesitated.

'I don't know. It's been a hectic few days and I'm tired.'

'Just a quick drink, please?'

Stanley came through the door.

'You could do with going out, love, relax a bit after the trauma of the last few days. We're nearly cleared up downstairs. I'll sweep the floor, Denise'll do the tables.'

He was lucky her parents always seemed keen for her to be in his company. Goodness knows why. She presumably hadn't told them about the Dora Perkins incident. Scott could see Jackie was reluctant and fully expected her to say no.

She nodded.

'OK. If you're sure.'

'I am, love. You've done more than your fair share here.'

'I'll go and get changed,' she said.

After she'd gone, Stanley turned to Scott.

'Thank you for offering to take her out. I do feel guilty that she's had to stay in Littlehampton. She'd planned to go back to Ipswich before Iris's appendicitis.'

'Had she?' He tried not to let the disappointment show in his voice. The depth of regret he felt surprised him. It went deeper than simply enjoying her company.

Stanley cleared Scott's dishes on to a tray and left.

'Are you ready?' Jackie was in the doorway, the jumper and boots reflecting the fact the weather wasn't so warm today.

'Yep. Let's go.'

It wasn't until she'd sat down at the

pub and he'd brought her over a half of cider that she blurted out what was on her mind.

'I found out from Val that the woman in the end house is called Dora Perkins and that's close enough to Doreen Parson, who you asked me about. So it can't be a coincidence. And you were definitely stalking her.'

In the last two days he'd not been able to work out what to tell Jackie about the whole sorry story. But the truth seemed as good an option as any.

'I know I should have been up front in the first place. I apologise about that. I wasn't stalking her, just trying to work out if she was the person I was looking for. But I'm sure she's too young.'

'But the name's different.'

'That's because I don't exactly know the name.'

She screwed up her face.

'I don't understand.'

'I probably shouldn't have asked you in the first place, but there was a possibility, however vague, that you might have a connection with her. You said your father was from here.'

She leant back.

'You've lost me, Scott.'

'Right. I have a half sister, but I don't remember her.'

Jackie opened her mouth in disbelief. Now he had her attention. It was a bit of a dramatic way to start, but that was the truth of it.

'We were separated in the war when I was less than a year old. We had the same mother, Kalina Lagodzinski.'

'Polish?'

'Yes. We had different fathers. My mother's first husband, my sister's father, perished early in the war. She then married my father, James Grant, and had me, but he was killed, too. In the Air Force.'

'Oh, Scott, I'm so sorry. And you said your mother died some years back.'

'A lot of years back. March the seventh, 1945, to be exact, in Bermondsey, during a V2 attack.'

Jackie clutched her chest.

'Oh, my goodness.'

'She was doing a shift as an ARP warden. My sister and I were being looked after by two different neighbours. When my mother died, my sister's paternal grandparents came to collect her before my father's parents even knew anything had occurred.'

'So what happened to you?'

'I was sent to an orphanage. It was only chance that my father left an address book at the house, with his belongings. In it the neighbour found the name Grant and assumed they were family. The neighbour contacted the police who went round to see my grandparents.'

Scott took a mouthful of his lager. He'd never told this story to anyone. It was harder even than he thought it would be.

'A bit of a shock for them, since they didn't know I existed before. My parents had a whirlwind affair, from what they could work out. They found a marriage certificate which told them my parents got married two weeks before my father was killed. They also found my birth

186

certificate. I was a honeymoon baby.'

'So your grandparents took you home.'

'Yes, to Wimbledon, where they still are. The neighbour looking after me was vague about my sister. All she knew was that her grandparents had taken her to the Littlehampton area. Everything that belonged to my sister had gone too. The neighbour thought she was called Doreen Parson, but couldn't be sure. The other neighbour, who'd looked after her, couldn't be located by that time. It was bedlam apparently, with the V2s, people missing, debris everywhere.'

'So what you're saying is, you're trying to find your sister. And you thought Dora Perkins could be her, if they got the name wrong.'

'Precisely.'

'You've never tried looking for her before?'

'I only found out about her two years ago, when I discovered a photo of the two of us in the attic.' The enormity of that discovery hit him anew.

'Your grandparents didn't tell you

about your sister?' Jackie shook her head.

'They thought it would be less traumatic if I didn't know.'

'What about your mother's parents? How come they didn't get involved?'

'No-one had any idea where they were. They might still have been in Poland. They might have died. Nobody knew.' He laughed drily. 'That's a whole other area of research.'

'Do you have that photo with you?'

'I do, and others my grandparents dug out. They're back at Mare Vista. I'll show you when we get back.'

'It's taken you two years to start looking for her?' It was almost an accusation.

'My career as an artist took off so I didn't have the time. But it gnawed at me, the thought of her being out there somewhere. When I came here the first time, I searched telephone directories, newspapers, anything I could get hold of that might give me a clue.'

'You've been going about it all the wrong way. Shouldn't you have gone to the records' office?'

He smiled. Telling her in the first place might have saved him a lot of bother. She was clearly a lot more clued up than him.

'I didn't realise that until I got home. Friends of my grandparents suggested St Catherine's House. I told my agent I needed to delay the exhibition for a personal matter. Luckily she was understanding.'

'So come on, what did you find out?'

Jackie had quite a different attitude to him now, which he was relieved about.

'It took me nearly two weeks because it turned out they'd spelled my mother's maiden name wrong on the marriage certificate. So neither surname I had was quite right. Finally, I tracked down a certificate for my mother's first marriage. After that, it was easier to track down the certificate for Maureen Pearson.'

Jackie let out a long sigh.

'Doreen Parson, Maureen Pearson. So close yet so far.'

'Indeed. I've been back through the directory but can't find an M Pearson.'

'If she's married, and she's likely to be, she won't be Pearson any more.'

'It's what I feared. So I'm back to square one. One of the Pearsons might be her grandparents, but I'm not sure how welcome a phone call from me would be.'

Jackie clutched her chin and narrowed her eyes.

'This is a long shot, but I found a 1963 directory in the understairs cupboard a while back. I left it there, so unless my parents have moved it . . .'

A new excitement stirred him.

'You never know. She'd have been twenty-one then and might have lived in a flat or something.'

'Come on then, drink up. Let's go and do some sleuthing.'

Unexpected Shock

When they'd got home from the pub, Jackie hadn't been able to find the directory in the understairs cupboard. Scott had been sorely disappointed, until Jackie promised to spend some time with him the next day, to work out what to do next.

They agreed to meet in the dining-room at 10 o'clock. Scott brought all his documents and photos down and laid them out on one of the bigger tables.

Jackie had a large book under her arm which she placed in a space on the table.

'Ta-da!' she announced.

'The 1963 directory! Where was it?'

'Dad had been having a clear out. Luckily the pile of rubbish hadn't got as far as the dustbin, but was sitting by the back door.'

He felt nervous.

'Have you looked?'

'Not yet.'

Taking a deep breath, Scott opened the directory in the middle, flicking the pages until he got to the Ps.

'Right, Pa . . . Pe . . . 'Pearson, A.' He ran his finger down. 'Pearson, M. There are three, two in Peacehaven, one in Arundel Road in Littlehampton.'

'That's just the other side of the town centre.'

'And the Arundel Road one says Miss M Pearson.' He could hardly breathe. Pearson wasn't a rare name, but still . . . it sounds promising.'

She must have noticed his hands were shaking.

'Tell you what, why don't I ring? They're more likely to trust a woman. They might think you're trying to stake the place out.'

'I hadn't even thought of that,' he said.

They went to the hall to ring the number.

'Hello,' Jackie said. 'I'm looking for a Maureen Pearson . . . Arundel Road . . . Ah, I see. OK. Thank you.' She put the phone down.

'That doesn't sound so promising.'

'The number must have been relocated as that man said he's in Maxwell Road.'

It was like struggling up a greasy pole, only to slither down again.

'We could go to the address in Arundel Road, knock on the door. See if whoever lives there knows anything.'

'I don't know.'

'What have you got to lose?' she asked.

'You're right. Let's do it now while I've still got the courage. How far is it?'

'Only ten, fifteen minutes' walk.'

'Come on, then.'

Jackie had already knocked on the door by the time Scott reached her on the path. The house was an imposing Victorian red brick building. Soon the door opened and there stood a middle-aged woman in a pinafore. She was too old to be Maureen, and too young to be her grandmother.

'If you're selling something, I don't buy from the door.'

'No, we're not,' Scott said. 'We're looking for a woman called Maureen

Pearson. She possibly used to live here.'

'Maureen Pearson, well, I never. We bought this house off her. Nineteen sixty-four, it was. If I remember rightly, her grandmother had died a couple of years before and she was getting married.'

'I don't suppose you have any idea where she moved to.'

'Does she owe money or something?' She crossed her arms.

'No, she's my sister,' Scott said. It still felt strange to say that. 'We've lost touch.'

'Well, let me see...' She stepped back. 'Ron?' she called. 'Do you remember where that Pearson girl moved to, the one we bought the house off?'

A man came to the door.

'Wickbourne Estate, wasn't it?'

'You're getting confused with your cousin.'

'That's all I can think of, I'm afraid.'

'Sorry we can't be any more help,' the woman said.

Scott's shoulders drooped.

'Thanks anyway.'

'The Wickbourne Estate's on the edge

of town,' Jackie said as they made their way back down the path, 'and leads to Wick, where Val and Dora Perkins live. My grandparents had a bungalow near there.'

'But they said she didn't move there.'

'No,' Jackie corrected. 'His wife said his cousin moved there. Doesn't mean Maureen didn't.'

It was a fair point.

'They said she was getting married, so she'll have a different surname. Where do we go from here?'

'It needs a little more thought. I've got to get back to do some cleaning now.'

'I'll take my canvas of the Arun down to the riverside and do some painting.'

* * *

Val waved at Jackie before she'd got two steps into the ward. She was sitting up in bed and looked far more cheerful than she'd done previously.

'Here, I've brought you a couple of magazines to read.' Jackie placed them on the bed.

'Fab! I could do with some more.' Val picked one up for a quick flick through.

'You look better today.'

'Yep. I told you I had a good feeling about things turning out for me, didn't I?'

'But you've just been knocked down.' Val leant forward cautiously.

'Exactly. And it led me here.'

'OK, you've lost me.'

'I've never really had any passion to follow a particular career, not until the last couple of days. Now I want to train as a nurse, helping people get well, like they have me. Especially Kitty.' She waved to a petite nurse who waved back.

'That's one heck of a way for fate to tell you where your path lies.'

'Yeah, I know it sounds a bit daft. Still, every cloud has a silver lining, as my mum's always keen on saying.'

It was great that Val felt so upbeat, given her melancholy mood the first few days she was in hospital.

'Well good luck to you. I'm glad you've

found your calling at last.' Jackie smiled to encourage her.

Val leant back and sighed happily.

'So am I. It's such a relief. And my parents are cock-a-hoop.'

Jackie was truly happy that Val had found a direction. She only wished she knew what she was going to do herself.

★ ★ ★

Jackie was clearing a breakfast table by the window. She listened as Scott chatted with Mrs Furst on the next table.

'Did you ever find your purse?' he asked, stirring his coffee.

'No, dear. Some scallywag's had that and no mistake.'

'I suppose you had to buy a new one.'

'Haven't got round to it yet,' she said. 'I was hoping it might turn up.'

Rita Watt had overheard.

'That's a shame. Now wait here a minute. I might be able to help you out.'

'Wonder what that's all about?' the old lady said. 'There you are, Archie, a nice sausage for you.' The Yorkshire terrier gave a few yips as she bent to give him his usual sausage from her plate.

Mrs Watt was soon back.

'There you go. I hope this will help you out.' She handed her a black purse. 'I have too many, as Raymond always tells me.' She glanced at him fondly and chuckled.

'Are you sure? It's very kind of you. Thank you.'

'It's nothing.' She shrugged coyly.

Raymond was soon by his wife's side.

'Better get going, pumpkin. We're heading into Bognor for the day. Toodle-loo.' They both waved and left.

Mrs Furst put some coins from a plastic bag into the new purse, then placed it on the table. Next she walked to the window while Archie enjoyed his treat.

'Looks a bit sunnier today. Think I'll have a walk by the river bank.'

As the old lady continued to stare out, Jackie's eye was caught by Scott leaning over to pick up the purse. She took a sharp intake of breath as she watched him place a five pound note inside.

Slowly letting out the breath, she looked back outside at the common, sweeping her gaze from the Beach Hotel to the funfair, as relief set in. She was seeing trouble where there wasn't any. A warm glow filled her. Five pounds was what Mrs Furst had lost with her purse. What a kind thing for Scott to do. She couldn't see Adrian doing anything like that.

She regretted the thought as she considered all the lovely things he'd paid for since they'd started dating. Yes, but because of that, he always expected to decide everything, where they went, what they did. And she wasn't that bothered about doing some of the expensive activities he'd taken her to. She was happy with a walk by the river, or visiting a park.

What an ungrateful girlfriend she'd been. Nevertheless, when she got back to Ipswich, she was determined to show him the pleasures of simple activities.

'Looks like Archie's finished,' Mrs

Furst said. 'I'll get ready to go out.' She went back to the table, scooped up her purse and Archie, and left.

'I was wondering if you had time to sit for me today,' Scott asked once the dining-room was empty.

'Not till after lunch. I'm cleaning all morning.'

'After lunch it is, then.'

★ ★ ★

Jackie sat for Scott for a couple of hours before both of them needed a rest. They decided to take his documents and photos and decamp to the Blue Sea, where Val had worked.

In the window of the café they sat with two frothy coffees, looking at the piece of paper that contained what they knew so far.

The waitress who'd served them, a young woman with black, curly hair, stood with her back against the ice-cream fridge, hands tucked into her green nylon overall. She was talking to the owner, an

Italian woman called Maria. At the table nearest the counter, a little girl was colouring in a book, her tongue sticking out in concentration.

Maria came over to their table.

'Hello. It's Jackie, isn't it? Any news about Val?'

'She's on the mend and being discharged today.'

'It was such a shock when you rang me,' Maria said. 'I sent a card and flowers along to the hospital, but do give her my best when you see her again.'

'I will,' Jackie said.

Maria returned to the counter.

Scott let out a frustrated moan.

'I'm running out of time. Eventually I'll have to get back to mount the exhibition. I can't delay it again.'

'I was wondering,' Jackie started, not sure how Scott would take her idea. 'Maybe you could put an ad in the 'Littlehampton Gazette'.'

He tapped his fingers on the table.

'It would be one way to do it. Maybe someone who knows her would see it, even if she didn't.'

'We could ring all the Pearsons on the off chance that one is a relative.'

'That was a last resort, but yes, it's coming to that. She might also have moved out of the area, but I'll never know if I don't try.'

Jackie was keen to solve this riddle and bring together a broken family. But . . . if they solved the puzzle, he wouldn't have a reason to remain at the guest house.

Scott leaned his elbows on the table, his chin resting on his hands. Jackie looked out of the window, watching as a large, grey ship sailed by.

They both sat upright when they heard the waitress call the little girl's name, their gaping disbelief turning from each other to the woman and child.

'Kalina, come and get a drink.'

'OK, Mummy.'

Scott went pale as he slowly brought his gaze back to Jackie. Her heart was pounding in her ears. If she felt like this, what must he feel like?

'That can't be coincidence, can it?'

he whispered. He had the look of someone haunted. Picking up the photo of
his mother holding him in her arms, he
looked from it to the woman.

'What do you think?' He handed the
image to her.

Jackie scrutinised the picture. There
was a similarity. It was hard to be sure
with the black and white image being so
old.

'She's got the same hair as you,' she
said. 'Why don't you ask her?'

'But she might know nothing about
me, like I did her.'

He had a point. It could be a massive
shock. And there was the child to con-
sider.

Scott stood, gathered the documents
and placed them back in his bag.

'I need to get out of here.'

Jackie followed as he rushed out. He
didn't stop until he reached the Nelson,
where he leant against the brick wall.

'I'm sorry,' he told her. 'I feel a little
sick.'

She pitied him. In his place she'd have

felt confused, maybe even frightened.

'What if she rejects me, Jackie?'

'You know where to find her now, if it is her. Let's go back and you can take your time to decide what to do next.'

'She must know her background at least if she's called her daughter Kalina.'

'What a shame Val's not in a position to find out a bit more for us.'

'I thought when I found her I'd tell her immediately. Now I just don't know.'

He pushed himself away from the wall and carried on round the corner. Jackie followed on.

Closer to the Truth

The following day, Jackie visited the café on her own. The aim was to find out something more about young Kalina's mother, to make sure she was who they thought she was.

Scott had decided to wait by the river and take photos.

When Jackie entered there were two waitresses serving, but there was no sign of the black-haired one from yesterday. Maria, the owner, was standing at the still machine, cleaning the steam pipe with a cloth.

'Hello again,' she said, spotting Jackie. 'How can I help you?'

'I was wondering,' she began, thinking on her feet. 'The waitress who served us yesterday. My friend thinks he recognises her from some years back. Is she by chance Maureen Pearson?'

Maria stopped cleaning and walked over, leaning on the ice-cream fridge.

'Bless him, he should have just asked

her. She doesn't bite. She's called Maureen right enough, but her surname's Swaden. Married to Jim Swaden, she is. No idea what her maiden name was.'

'She's not here today, I suppose.'

'No, it's her day off. Only does Monday to Thursday.'

'That's a shame.'

'I guess Maureen didn't recognise your friend then, or she was unsure, like him.'

'It has been a good number of years, like I said.'

'Oh, I've just remembered that she's half Polish, if that helps,' Maria said.

'Yes, Scott did mention that.'

'Got a lovely house on the Wickbourne Estate, one of the self-builds. And Kalina's a lovely little girl, named after the Polish grandmother, I believe. Killed in the war she was.

'Maureen had to bring Kalina in yesterday because her mother-in-law had to go out. She'll be in on Monday, nine till three, if your friend would like to pop back.'

'Thank you, Maria, he may well do that.'

Outside once more, she quickly crossed the road then jumped down the wall on to the concrete bank. Scott was standing near the edge, looking over the river to the yachts stranded on the bank on the other side. He twisted around, eyes wide with hope and enquiry.

'She's not in today but she's called Maureen Swaden now and lives on the Wickbourne Estate. That's the estate that couple in Arundel Road mentioned.'

'So you think it is her?'

'Maria said Kalina's named after Maureen's Polish mother.'

Scott looked away into the distance, his hands shaking as they gripped his camera.

'Are you OK?'

'I — I don't know.' He shuddered, as if waking from a dream. 'Yes, I'll be OK.'

'It's just, I've got to go and help Dad with the cleaning now.'

'Of course. I'll carry on taking photos of the river, perhaps take the ferry to the other side. I won't do anything about Maureen until you have more time. If that's OK?'

'It's more than OK, Scott. I'm busy at the weekend, including going to see Val and taking Mum out. I'll be free next on Monday.'

He nodded.

'You get along now. I know your dad really appreciates all the extra help you've given.'

They walked back to the wall and hauled themselves up. Scott headed towards the ferry while she went the opposite way. She looked back at him as he trudged down Pier Road.

Inside her head swirled a mixture of emotions — sympathy, worry, admiration. And possibly something else. She had no time, or inclination, to examine it now.

★　★　★

'I want to do some washing up,' Iris complained from her place on the settee. 'I'm bored with the TV and reading.'

'Well, you can't.' Stanley looked down at his wife life like a protective father. 'It's not even four weeks yet since the operation.'

Jackie felt sorry for her mother. She'd have got bored too, sitting down all day.

'You should be grateful for the opportunity to have time off,' he said.

'You know I've never been an idle person, Stanley Harris. And if I was having time off I'd rather be on holiday somewhere.'

'Couldn't she sit in a dining chair by the draining board and do some drying up?' Jackie suggested.

Stanley huffed.

'I suppose so. Denise, bring a chair here, would you? I'll help your mother over.'

Denise put down her tea towel and did as she was asked.

Iris stood up.

'For goodness' sake, I can manage by

209

myself.'

Jackie could imagine Val being like that at home.

'I'd better go and see if Mrs Furst has appeared. It's not like her to be down last for breakfast.'

As she entered the dining-room, she heard a clattering down the stairs, along with a repeated mumbled: 'Oh dear, oh dear.'

Jackie looked up to see the old lady, her downturned mouth and sad eyes suggesting she was about to cry.

'You haven't lost your purse again, have you, Mrs Furst?'

She reached the ground floor out of breath.

'Yes, and I was so busy looking for it that I forgot I'd left the door open. Archie escaped. And the front door's been left open.' Her voice reached a crescendo as she pointed to it.

Some new guests had not long gone out and must have forgotten to close it.

Scott was soon in the hall.

'I heard what you said. I'll go and look

for him, over on the common.'

He went quickly to his table, wrapping something in a napkin before running down the concrete steps.

'We've finished so we'll go, too,' Rita Watts said. 'We'll cover the pavement between here and the river. I'll just go and fetch our jackets.'

Rita ran upstairs while Raymond looked at himself in the mirror to neaten first his moustache, then his cravat.

There was only one other couple left in the dining-room, a young pair holding hands at the table in the corner.

'You sit down, Mrs Furst,' Jackie said. 'I'll get Denise to cover me so I can help with the search.'

Her sister was fond of Archie and would want him to be found as soon as possible.

'I'm not sure I could eat anything.' Her voice was shaking.

'At least have a cup of tea to calm your nerves.'

Mrs Furst nodded and took a seat at her usual table.

Having sorted Denise out, Jackie left. She spotted Scott halfway across the common and waved before running over to him. He was calling Archie's name and had the napkin in his hand with a sausage poking out. Probably wanted to finish his breakfast.

'I'll go and check the beach,' she said. 'Could be the little scamp fancied a swim.'

'I'll carry on along the common and head to the pond.'

Jackie went on her way, looking round all the while. The term 'needle in a haystack' came to mind. The area was vast and Archie very small. He was also fast. He might be halfway to Rustington by now, or to town.

There were all those side roads he could have gone down, which gave an ample opportunity for him to be run over. Like Val.

Jackie was almost crying by the time she got to the beach, imagining poor little Archie coming to grief. Mrs Furst would be heartbroken if that happened.

Jackie made her way down to the pier first, all the time scanning the area. The beach was nearly empty, being early. That at least might help locate a small dog.

She'd walked up and down twice, from the pier to Mewsbrook Park, before coming to the conclusion it was useless. Coming halfway back along the promenade, she set off across the common, dejected.

Back at Mare Vista she drooped as she put the key in the lock. Inside she heard a fuss coming from the dining-room, thinking at first it was an argument.

It soon became clear it was nothing of the sort. Archie was jumping and turning around, excited by all the fuss he was clearly getting. Calling cheers of encouragement were Scott, Stanley and Denise.

'He came back?' Jackie said.

Mrs Furst put her arm through Scott's.

'No. This ingenious young man lured him.'

'Ingenious?' Jackie wondered what on earth he'd done.

'I wouldn't call it ingenious,' Scott said. 'I guessed Archie might smell the sausage if he was nearby. It certainly helped me catch him once I spotted him.'

'Oh — the sausage was for Archie.' Jackie put her head back and laughed.

Mrs Furst pulled her purse from her cardigan pocket. From it she extracted a five pound note.

'Here you are, young man. Your reward for finding Archie.'

Scott shook his head, waving his hand to confirm his resolve.

'Thank you but no. I was only too glad to help.'

Mrs Furst returned the note to her purse.

'You are a lovely young man. Have you a girlfriend?'

He glanced at Jackie.

'No, I haven't. Are you offering, Mrs Furst?'

The old lady giggled.

'If I were fifty years younger. Now, I wonder what's happened to Rita and Raymond. I hope they don't spend too much time looking.'

Could This be the Answer?

Scott was the last one left at breakfast on Monday, staring out of the window from his table on the opposite wall. Jackie was clearing the table by the fireplace, one eye on him and one on the cloudy day.

Scott spoke suddenly, making her jump.

'I need to look in the directory again, to get Maureen's phone number. I've been tempted every time I've passed it, but the closer I get, the more scared I feel.'

'Let me take this downstairs and help clear up, then I'll meet you in here about ten? I've got most of today free as I got ahead yesterday and Dad's already on top of dinner.'

He nodded.

'By the way . . . ' He paused, pressing his lips together.

'Yes?'

'I don't know if I should say this . . . When I was searching for Archie, I got down to the river and had a quick look down Pier Road before doubling back. The Watts said they'd cover the pavement down to the river, but they were sitting in the window of the Sea Breezes, drinking coffee. They didn't notice me.'

'Really? They claimed to have searched down each side road on the way down, and then walked into town.'

'I don't want to cause trouble. Just thought it a bit odd.'

'It is. At least we got Archie back, or rather, you did.' She gave him a warm smile.

He shrugged in his usual modest way. 'We have the sausage to thank.'

She laughed out loud.

'Oh, Scott, can't you take praise?'

'That's what my agent says. I guess I always feel I haven't tried hard enough.'

It was a brief glimpse into a deep insecurity. Jackie wondered if his family history was at the heart of it.

'Better to be like that than thinking you're marvellous for every little thing you do.'

Adrian flashed into her mind. He hadn't phoned for a few days, miffed as he was that she was still in Sussex.

Scott made eye contact and her stomach flipped. There was such a depth in them, displaying a mixture of vulnerable emotions. Adrian's eyes were harder to read, unless he was angry.

'I'll get this sorted out then. The quicker I do that the quicker I'll be back.'

'Jackie.'

She came to a halt.

'Thank you,' he said.

'What for?'

'Helping me out. And being understanding. It's helped having someone to share this with.'

'You're welcome.'

She carried on through the door as an urge to cry overtook her. She wasn't sure why, but reined it in before she got downstairs to her parents.

★　★　★

On the dining table by the window, Jackie and Scott sat next to each other with the directory open in front of them.

'There are three Swadens on the Wickbourne Estate, but none with the initial J.'

Scott clutched his chin and looked thoughtful.

'Perhaps Jim's a nickname, or James is his second name?'

'Or they don't have a phone. It might be worth ringing the others as they might know. Failing that, you could catch her as she leaves work, that way it wouldn't be in front of the staff or customers. I'd come with you.'

'It still doesn't seem the right approach.'

'We can't do anything till later. Why don't we go for a walk? Or you could paint and I could watch.'

He raised his eyebrows.

'Are you trying to distract me?'

'No point fretting all day.'

'True. But I think you'd get mighty bored just watching me. Do you still have any sketch pads, paints, pencils, anything?'

'I have them all. But it's been years since I drew properly.'

'Let's take our sketch books out and we can work together.'

That was a scary thought.

'I'm not up to it.'

'Think of it as a master class, then.'

The idea appealed more than she liked to admit.

'OK. Where would you like to go?'

'The beach, near the pier and kiosks. There's plenty to work on there.'

Jackie looked forward to indulging in her little hobby, as Adrian had unkindly put it. But overlaying that was the anticipation of spending another day with Scott.

* * *

Jackie and Scott had settled themselves on the promenade between the beach and 1950s kiosks. Between Scott's shooting stool and Jackie's folding chair was a small table with a paintbox and water.

He was facing one way, sketching the pier, she the other, painting the kiosks.

He glanced over at her creation every now and again to compliment and make suggestions. It reminded her of those times at school, in the art room. They were always sunny in her head, though probably not in reality. More likely she remembered them like that because they were so special and she missed them.

'You've stopped painting,' Scott said, taking a break from his own picture.

'I was remembering my school days. You seem calmer now.'

'Being creative has always helped still my mind. That's why I suggested it.'

'My granny used to say the same about knitting.'

'My gran knits, too. Makes up the patterns herself. Reckon my artistic gene might come from her. Though it's possible it came from my mother's side. I wouldn't know, would I?'

He looked sad once more. What must it be like to have a complete blank with half your family? Jackie patted his arm, her hand lingering there a few seconds after.

'Come on, let's get a bit more done,' he said. 'You're doing very well for someone who's supposedly rusty. I can see already you have talent.'

'Get away with you. I've only painted a few kiosks with some balls, buckets and spades.'

'You have a good eye for detail, a great sense of colour and an interesting style.'

'Thank you,' she said, suspecting that 'interesting' was a polite term for 'odd'.

They carried on with their own pictures. She soon realised he was humming 'Could It Be Forever?' She'd heard it on the radio earlier so it was possible he had too.

Could it be for ever, her life back in Ipswich with Adrian? It was something she needed to work out before she moved on to the next phase of her life.

★　★　★

'Shall I ring this first one, see where it gets us?' Jackie pointed at the C. Swaden on the directory. It felt like déjà vu after trying to find her own sister.

'Would you? Like you said before, they might react better to a woman ringing.'

She picked up the receiver and dialled the first number.

'Oh, hello. I was wondering if Maureen Swaden was there.'

'Who's calling?' a female voice asked.

A jolt of excitement went through her. This was promising.

'A friend from years ago. I'm trying to get hold of her.'

Scott's eyes stretched wide.

'She doesn't live here.'

'Would you be able to tell me where she is, please?'

'No, I couldn't. I don't know who she is.'

Before Jackie had a chance to say anything, the phone was disconnected.

'Oh, dear, she's not very trusting. I'm sure she did know her from her initial reaction.'

'Perhaps she's had a bad experience in the past.' He looked disappointed.

'I'll try the next number.'

The second voice, also a woman's, was friendlier in its greeting. Jackie decided on a different approach.

'Hello, my name's Jackie Harris and I'm trying to locate Maureen Swaden, formerly Maureen Pearson, for a family member.'

She peered up at Scott, hoping he'd approve. He nodded and seemed OK about her approach.

'She doesn't live here, but my husband is her husband's cousin.'

'Would you be able to give me a number for her, please?'

Scott gripped his hands together, his face hopeful.

'Let's see,' the woman said, 'I've got it somewhere. Or you could find it in the directory under P. Swaden, Belloc Road.'

'Hold on.' Jackie ran her finger down the column of names. 'Yes, here it is. I thought her husband was called Jim.'

'He uses his middle name.'

'Thank you so much, you don't know how helpful you've been.'

'I know she's short of family since her grandparents died, so it can't hurt.'

They said their goodbyes and Jackie placed the phone down.

'It's one of the numbers in the book?' Scott asked.

'P. Swaden. You were right, Jim uses a middle name.'

Jackie went to pick the receiver up once more but Scott put his hand over hers.

'Don't you want me to ring her?'

'I think it's time I did this for myself.'

She offered up the receiver then pointed to the number in the directory as he dialled.

The ongoing purring tones of the other phone convinced Scott that no-one was at home. He bit his bottom lip. Jackie was twisting her hair and biting her lip as she watched him. He was deeply touched by her concern.

He was about to replace the receiver when a woman's voice spoke.

'Hello.'

At first he couldn't speak.

'Hello?' she repeated.

'Hello. Is that Maureen Swaden, formerly Pearson?'

'Who wants to know?' It was a challenge.

'You may not have heard of me, but my name's Scott Grant and I think you may be my sister.'

There was a gasp on the other end of the line before the sound of sobbing.

'Are you all right?' he asked.

'Oh, Scott, I've been waiting years for this phone call,' came the shaky reply.

His chin wobbled as the tears escaped his eyes.

'I didn't know you existed until two years ago.'

Jackie walked away and down the stairs. He was grateful for the privacy.

'I vaguely remember you,' she said. 'I asked my grandparents about you but they said you must be a friend's baby. I didn't realise you were my brother until my aunt told me the truth five years ago.'

'Can I come and visit you?' It was an abrupt request. She may not be ready.

'As soon as you can. Where are you? Do you still live in London?'

'I live in Wimbledon, but I'm currently staying in Littlehampton, at a guest house.'

'Then come today, please. Let's not waste any more time.'

⋆ ⋆ ⋆

Jackie drove Scott to Belloc Road, stopping outside a semi-detached house. Scott stared at it for a few moments, unmoving.

'You know she wants to see you, Scott,' Jackie said to encourage him.

'It's still daunting. What if we don't get on?'

'Only one way to find out.'

He pushed the door open and stepped out.

'I'll walk back.' He smiled weakly.

'Good luck.'

She watched as he opened the black metal gate and made his way down the drive. No sooner had he lifted his hand to knock at the door, than Maureen stepped out and took Scott in her arms.

Jackie experienced a brief spell of envy. By the time she drove away, a new optimism had taken over. Anything seemed possible to her at that moment.

Back outside Mare Vista, she found a police car in their usual space and had to park next door.

'Goodness me, what now?' She ran up the steps and crashed into the hall. There were voices coming from the sitting-room. She entered to find the Watts sitting together on a settee. Her father and two police officers were standing.

'What on earth is going on?' she said.

'This is my daughter,' Stanley explained.

'It's all a horrible mistake, or a set-up.' Rita Watt was indignant.

'I can assure you it isn't,' the sergeant said. 'Caught red-handed in town you were. And look at all these, found in your room.' He pointed to a large collection of purses and wallets on the coffee table, plus a couple of handbags.

Jackie stared at the ill-gotten gains.

'They've been purse-snatching?'

'One to distract, one to snatch.' Stanley folded his arms and glared.

'You make it sound so tawdry,' Raymond said.

Jackie went forward and pointed to the bright green purse.

'This is Mrs Furst's purse. You couldn't even leave the old lady you'd befriended alone?'

Rita put her head in the air and pouted, while Raymond looked ahead, expressionless.

'And the one you gave Mrs Furst must have been stolen, too.'

'If there's another purse, we'd better have that, too,' the sergeant said.

Jackie was about to leave to tell Mrs Furst what had happened when the old lady came through the door. The offending item was held aloft in one hand, while the other clutched Archie.

'Denise came and told me what's happened. I guess you'll be needing this.'

Archie, spotting the Watts, yapped for

all he was worth.

'Quiet boy, quiet now.'

He gave a little growl by way of a post-script.

'You can have your own one back in due course,' the sergeant said. 'In the meantime, we need to get these two down the station and charged.'

The pair were escorted outside, Mrs Watts struggling and trying to make it as hard as possible for the constable. When they'd gone, Stanley turned to Jackie.

'Well, who'd have thought it, eh? Refined Rita and dapper Raymond.'

'Reduced circumstances, no doubt,' Mrs Furst said. 'I feel a bit sorry for them, really.'

'I don't.' Stanley snorted. 'To think they may have been paying us with sto-len money.'

They looked through the dining-room window as the police car drove away.

Impatient Visitor

Scott hadn't returned for dinner. Maybe Maureen had asked him to stay for the rest of his time in Littlehampton. Jackie tried not to feel disappointed at this possibility. If they'd hit it off that much, it would be wonderful.

Currently Val's dad was helping her to the settee in the guest sitting-room. Her friend had only been home four days, but had phoned earlier to bemoan her 'imprisonment', as she saw it. Wanting to help out, Jackie had invited Val over, deciding it would be a distraction for her, too.

'I'll leave you to it then,' Mr Matthews said. 'I'll be back ten-thirty. That gives you a good couple of hours.'

'Thanks, Dad, you're a star,' Val said.

He left and the girls settled down to chat, getting the Watts' arrest over and done with first.

'You said something about Scott tracing his sister?' Val still wasn't convinced of his good character.

'It turned out that the sneaking around was only because he didn't want to alarm her. Sensible, really, even if it wasn't the right way to go about it.'

'I'll say. I had him pegged as a mugger, or worse.'

'Val! No, he's all right. It can't be easy, being orphaned so young.'

'No, I guess not.'

They heard a car engine outside. Jackie jumped up and looked through the window. Scott was getting out of a Mini.

'Hold on a mo,' she told Val.

Out in the hall she met Scott coming in.

'Looks like it went well,' she said, noting the relaxed smile.

'Shall we sit down and I'll tell you all about it?'

'Val's here for a couple of hours,' she whispered. 'If you want to tell me later instead.'

He looked crestfallen for a moment, then seemed to buck up.

'I don't mind if she hears.'

He followed Jackie into the sitting-room, greeting Val and asking how she was.

'I'm on the mend, ta. How did you get on?'

'Great. Got a few questions answered.' His next words tumbled out. 'It turns out Maureen and I were taken to different orphanages after they discovered my mother had died. Maureen's grandparents thought I must have perished, too, and didn't want to upset her.

'Years later, visiting the area to see how it had been rebuilt, they got speaking to a local who turned out to be another neighbour of my mother's. It was then they discovered I'd survived, but had no way of knowing where I was.'

He took a deep breath, in which time Val asked, 'So, what happened next?'

'Not a lot. Maureen's grandparents never felt it was the right time to tell her. After they died, an aunt who felt she should know told her. But she had no idea how to find out about me and was pregnant with Kalina by then. It's weird to think I'm an uncle.' He chuckled.

'Are you spending time with them while you're here?' It was Jackie's subtle way of finding out whether he was going to stay with them.

'Not this time. Could I have a word about that?' He indicated the hall.

As Scott left the room, Val winked at Jackie. Goodness knows what she thought Scott's intentions were.

'I've got to get back to London tomorrow,' he said once they were in the hall.

She wasn't ready for him to go yet.

'Of course. But what about your sister?'

'She's not going anywhere, and I've got to knuckle down for this exhibition. However, I am returning in September to stay with her.'

'Wonderful. It couldn't have worked out better.' Even as she said this, a little piece of her heart got chipped away. She was so much fonder of him than she should be.

The doorbell rang. Jackie cursed the interruption.

'I'd better go and pack. I'm catching an early train tomorrow. I rang your dad earlier to tell him my plans and he's going to drive me to the station.'

That must have been the phone call while she was serving dinner. Dad had answered it but they were so busy he'd not said what it was about.

The doorbell rang again, more insistently.

'I'll speak to you later,' Scott said.

She didn't bother trying to identify the impatient visitor through the glass before pulling the door open.

'About time.'

It was Adrian.

Finding 'The One'

Adrian was the last person Jackie wanted to see at this moment in time.

'What took so long? I could see you through the glass.'

'What are you doing here, Adrian?'

'That's a nice way to greet your boy-friend.'

'Adrian, you're not . . . '

'Since you seem to be stuck here, I've come to rescue you.'

'What?'

Jackie spotted Val at the sitting-room door, a crutch under each arm.

'It was a last minute decision and you know I'm not normally rash.'

'No, not rash enough most times.'

He looked confused by her statement.

'Anyway . . . ' He fell on one knee. 'Will you marry me?'

'What?' Jackie and Val exclaimed to-gether, alerting Adrian to Val's presence.

'No, Adrian, I won't.'

Val did a silent clap and cheer.

'What?' He looked like someone who'd been slapped. 'Isn't that what you want?'

'You know what? It isn't. It's taken me a while to realise that. We've had some good times, but you're just not 'the one'. And admit it, you simply don't like being left behind. You always have to be the winner.'

He rose hastily.

'Well! If that's how you feel.'

'It is.'

'You'll come running back, just wait and see.' With that, he stalked off to his car.

'Well done.' Val grinned.

'I'm not sure I should have been so blunt.'

'It was a long time coming, if you ask me.'

About to close the door, Jackie noticed Gary reach the steps.

'Watcha,' he said. 'Did you see me coming?'

'Not exactly.' She looked over to where Adrian was fiddling with the lock of his car.

'I went to Val's house and I gather she's here.'

'That's right. Come in.'

In a flash Adrian was rushing back along the pavement.

'So you've got a new boyfriend already?' He reached the top step at the same time as Gary. 'You go for scruffy urchins now, do you?' He indicated the long blond hair, worn denim jacket and loons.

'Chill out, man, you'll bust a gasket,' Gary said.

Jackie's head was thumping, she was so cross.

'Gary is here to see Val. And I'll thank you not to be rude to my friends. As for running back to you, I can assure you that won't happen.

'Adrian, you are a rude, big-headed clot who thinks throwing his money and weight around will get him whatever he wants. Well, it won't get me. I'm staying here and going to . . . going to . . . '

What was she going to do?

'I'm going to apply to teacher training

college in Chichester and do art as my subject. It's what I should have done in the first place.' Where had that come from? It must have been simmering in her mind since Val mentioned the college.

Adrian looked stunned.

'I'm sorry,' she added, 'but only for not breaking it off properly when I left. It was a mistake leaving the relationship open.'

Adrian descended the steps meekly.

Jackie turned her attention to Gary.

'Come in.' It was only then she wondered why he'd come to see Val and not her.

In the hall he smiled to see Val there.

'Watcha. How you doing now?'

'I had to get out of the house. I'm being treated like a child. What are you doing here?' She pressed her lips together.

'Your mum said you were here. I wanted a word.'

'You came to see me?'

'Why don't you go in the sitting-room,' Jackie said. 'I'll fetch you a drink,

238

Gary.'

'No, no, gotta say it now or I'll lose my bottle again. Valerie, will you go out with me? Please?'

Val's mouth opened in shock.

'I thought you liked Jackie.'

'I do — as a mate. I thought you were into Stuart, till he told me he's been trying to get us two together.'

'Has he?'

'Well?'

Jackie was as eager to hear the answer as Gary. She willed Val to say yes.

'Yeah, course I'll go out with you.'

Gary stepped forward as excited as a puppy and put his arm gently round Val's shoulder.

'Actually a cuppa tea sounds great now.'

'Coming up. You two have a sit down.'

Jackie was passing the stairs when she saw Scott heading down the last flight.

'What's all the noise about?'

Val's voice piped up from the doorway.

'Adrian asked Jackie to marry him.'

Scott's face fell.

'Seriously?'

'Yes. And I said no.'

'Very firmly,' Val called, disappearing through the door.

'I'm glad to hear it,' Scott said. 'I mean, because I never thought he seemed the one for you. On the short acquaintance I made with him. And from what you said.'

Jackie wondered why he was over explaining. Still, he was right.

'Only I couldn't see it, apparently.'

'Sorry, it wasn't a criticism,' he said.

'I didn't take it as one. Mum and Dad have said the same. Even Aunty Brenda did.'

'What are you going to do?'

She hesitated, wondering if he'd think her overconfident in her choice of career.

'I'm, um, going to apply to teacher training college in Chichester and do — art.'

His grin was broad. He took hold of both her arms.

'That's marvellous. So you're staying in the area.'

'In Littlehampton, yes.'

'Good for you. I'm really pleased.'

'Who knows, we might bump into each other when you're down visiting your sister.' It was feeling increasingly unlikely to her, which saddened her much more than she thought possible.

'Didn't I tell you I've booked at least two weeks at Mare Vista in September? I don't want to crowd my sister and her family. And I'd love to do more sketches and paintings of the area. It's my new favourite place.'

Jackie's mood lifted so instantly it was as if she'd taken flight just above the ground.

'That's great. Yeah. Really great.' She resisted doing a little jig.

'And I'd like to see you again, of course. We've had fun and I've enjoyed your company.'

'Likewise,' she said.

'And not many people would give up so much of their precious time to help someone, like you did. I'm really grateful. Thank you.'

Neither of them knew what to do next, until at the same time, they both lunged forward for a hug. They giggled as they almost crashed into each other. After a long moment they parted, still holding hands.

'If it's OK with you, I'm going to put that painting of you in the exhibition.'

'How exciting.'

'And after, it'll be a gift of appreciation.'

She felt her face flush.

'I don't know what to say.'

'You don't have to say a thing.' It was almost a whisper. 'And,' he added, 'I'll make sure you get an invitation to see the exhibition. If you'd like.'

'I would like. So you're off after breakfast tomorrow?'

'Yes. Hopefully the time will fly till September. I'll look forward to it.'

'I'll look forward to it too.'